Nathan Kaldwell has been a deputy in the town of Stone Ridge for many years. In that time, he's noticed a few peculiarities in many of the town's occupants. Since the occupants' oddities never seem to pose a danger to anyone, Nathan keeps the information to himself. When a motorcycle gang comes to town, being a bike enthusiast, he stops to admire their rides.

To Nathan's surprise, what he thinks is a large gray dog in a sidecar turns out to be a wolf. A shocking series of events reveals that the wolf is also a man named Khan, a paranormal creature called a shifter. While Nathan's attracted to the pretty man, he spots the tell-tale signs of a wounded and abused soul. He's not certain if even what the shifters call the mate-pull can convince the skittish Khan to stay in human form for him.

When Nathan learns there's shifter hunters in the area, can he keep Khan safe in either form?

Skittish Seduction
Copyright © 2023 Charlie Richards
ISBN: 978-1-4874-4002-2
Cover art by Angela Waters

Published by eXtasy Books Inc

Look for us online at:
www.eXtasybooks.com

Skittish Seduction
Wolves of Stone Ridge 62

By

Charlie Richards

DEDICATION

Feel the fear and do it anyway.
~Susan Jeffers

PROLOGUE

"Hey, Khan."

The wolf known as Khan turned his head and peered up at Adam. Khan wasn't his original name, but when Payson had dubbed him with it, he'd been happy to answer to it. In fact, when Payson had shown him the *Star Trek* movie that starred the character in it, even though he was technically a bad guy, Khan decided to keep the name. While it was probably a little silly, he hoped that by taking the enhanced human's name, he could take on a little of the guy's strength.

That Khan was a badass.

Focusing on Adam, Khan yipped softly in greeting to the white tiger shifter who'd stopped in front of him.

"It's time to head out. You ready to go to Stone Ridge with us?" Adam glanced around the clearing as he rested his hands on his hips before returning his attention to Khan, a grin curving the blond man's lips. "Or did you decide to stay in the bayou with some of the others?"

Just like every shifter who Alpha Kontra Belikov had either rescued from scientists or had been offered for rehabilitation by the Four Horsemen of the Apocalypse after they'd been rescued from witches, Khan had been given a choice—continue under his protection and go to Stone Ridge with them or stay with Olson, who owned the Victorian they'd been staying at, as well as Olson's shifter mate, Able. The fae and their mates were staying, as well, at least for a time. Although, since fae didn't actually age, their idea of *for a time* could have been for a couple of centuries.

1

Who knows.

Dipping his canine snout in a quick nod, Khan confirmed his desire to stay with Kontra. That would keep him with fellow wolf shifters, Vail and Ishmael, too. Khan enjoyed running with the mated shifters.

To everyone's surprise, another wolf shifter, Diego — Vail's grandfather — had chosen to stay. He hadn't wanted to intrude on another wolf alpha's territory. Plus, his zebra shifter mate, Zack, had become really great friends with the fae prince, Elroy. Diego hadn't dreamed of separating them.

Such a sweet guy. Wonder if I'll ever find a handsome dominant mate who'll be so sweet to me.

I'd have to shift and be in human form for that, though.

While Khan had never revealed it to anyone there, he *had* shifted into his human form a couple of times. He never stayed in it for long because it made him feel so vulnerable. In wolf form, Khan had teeth and claws, and his four paws could carry him away from danger far faster than two human feet could.

"Glad to hear it," Adam told him, giving him a scratch on the shoulder. "You gonna try to shift, so you can come as a human?" Cocking his head, Adam told him, "You could ride on the back of Lamar's *Goldwing*. I've heard it's damn comfortable."

Khan did a fantastic job of rolling his eyes in wolf form, causing Adam to laugh.

"All right, all right." Adam smirked. "You get a choice then. One of the motorcycle trailers or the sidecar?"

Glancing between the offered options, Khan quickly decided. The guys had renovated a pair of motorcycle trailers, giving them windows for air circulation. They'd also installed an intercom for communication, as well as a handle so they could open the hatch themselves.

Well, most of the shifters could.

Khan didn't think the coral snake shifter would be able to

handle the latch, but he could just go out the window.

Moving to the side car that was attached to Beta Sam's large bike, Khan yipped and sat beside it. There were two other options, but he didn't feel comfortable riding with Draven. The man was a warlock, and feeling his magick always left his fur tingling. The rhino shifter, Aaron, had already claimed the sidecar attached to Mutegi's motorcycle.

"You got it, Khan," Adam patted him again before waving at the car. "Hop in."

Khan did as instructed and hopped into the car, sitting on the seat.

"Hey, Khan," Sam greeted as he stopped at his motorcycle. "You with me, then. Huh?"

Giving the beta a canine grin and a yip, Khan acknowledged the Texas longhorn shifter's words.

"Well, if that's the case, you need a helmet," Sam told him. To Khan's surprise, the beta pulled a small black helmet with goggles attached from his saddlebags. "Draven had a vision," he told him, answering Khan's unspoken question. As Sam fitted the helmet to Khan, he told him, "He ordered it online and picked it up from the post office yesterday."

Khan chuffed, his version of a canine laugh. Other than that, he held still for Sam's ministrations, letting the big beta shifter strap it onto his wolf's head.

"All right, everyone," Kontra called, his loud voice carrying across the yard. "Mount up."

The men milling around the yard said their last goodbyes to their friends before doing as the alpha ordered. The roar of motorcycle engines filled the air.

Then Sam started them forward, and Khan felt the wind ruffle his fur as he went for his first motorcycle ride.

CHAPTER ONE

Nathan Kaldwell tipped his hat at Sheriff Anthony Holsteen as he made his way out of the sheriff's station. "Afternoon, sheriff," he greeted.

"Have a safe shift," Anthony told him before picking up the ringing phone.

Nodding, Nathan let himself out of the station as he thought about how their prior sheriff would never have lowered himself to answering the dispatcher phones. That man had been a pompous ass and had considered it beneath him. Anthony, on the other hand, did every task that he expected his deputies under him to do, including cleaning. Nathan respected the hell out of the man for that.

Nathan turned left and began walking around the building. As he made his way to the back alley, he thought about the changes that had taken place over the last year.

The old sheriff had finally retired—forced out, really, from the rumors Nathan had heard. He'd learned that Anthony was the brother of Dixon, one of their newer park rangers. The rangers used some pull with the mayor to get Anthony the sheriff's position.

Nathan appreciated the change. The first thing Anthony had done was fire Michelle, their long-time front desk receptionist. She'd been a toxic, bigoted woman who'd been blackmailing the prior sheriff. Although, Nathan had never heard what she had on him.

As Nathan paused in the alley behind the building, he took in the back of the buildings and the cars in the parking lots.

4

He spotted Lizzie holding her one-year-old daughter, opening her car door. With a wave, Nathan greeted them, then began moving along the backs of the buildings.

There wasn't a whole lot of crime in Stone Ridge, and the vibe of the town was relaxed and friendly. Nathan liked it, and he patrolled on foot to keep it that way. There were plenty of tourists who frequented the town to take advantage of the hiking and camping available in the nearby national forest. Seeing a man in uniform strolling through town often stopped problems before they could even start.

Moving swiftly, Nathan made it down the street and turned left onto Main. He peered left and right, seeing the normal flow of people coming and going from the local grocery store, bank, and other establishments. Some people he recognized and some he didn't.

Nathan headed toward the back alleys once more. Some of the shops on Main Street had apartments over the top of them. They were mostly used by the busy shopkeepers or younger singles moving out on their own for the first time. He liked to make certain everyone's place was in good repair. Liking to keep busy, Nathan occasionally offered to help if anyone needed assistance with any upkeep.

"Hey, Maddy." Nathan greeted the older woman who owned the bookshop. The woman was shuffling forward, holding a garbage bag, so he hurried toward her. "Can I help you with that?"

"Oh, thank you, deputy," Maddy responded, smiling widely. "You're so kind."

Taking the bag from her, Nathan returned her smile. "It's my pleasure," he told her before crossing to the dumpster.

After disposing of the bag, Nathan turned back and tipped his hat at her. "You have a great day, Maddy," he told her.

"My granddaughter is coming into town this weekend," Maddy told him, her blue eyes dancing with mischief. "She's about your age, and she's single." With a girlish giggle, Maddy told him, "I'd be happy to introduce you."

Nathan did his best to hide his mental wince. "Uh, it's awfully kind of you to think of me, Maddy, but—" Pausing, he racked his mind for a suitable response and came up with, "Uh, I'm not in a position to pursue a relationship." Offering Maddy a rakish grin, Nathan spread his arms and quipped, "Work is my mistress and all that." As he spoke, he began moving away from her.

"You're not getting any younger, Deputy Nathan," Maddy told him. Cocking her head, she surprised him by claiming, "I have a grandson, too. Maybe he'd be more to your liking."

Barking a laugh, Nathan shook his head. "I'll find my special someone someday," he told her with a shrug. He'd never hidden the fact that he was bisexual, but he'd never had anyone try to set him up with a guy before. "When the right person comes along, I'll know."

"How will you know if you don't meet new people?" Maddy pressed, staring at him questioningly.

Nathan bit back a sigh, desperately wanting out of the conversation. "Uh, I'd best be getting on with my patrols, Maddy," he told her, deciding using work as an excuse was best. When Maddy still looked like she would press, Nathan added, "When your granddaughter arrives, I'm sure we'll cross paths at some point."

Then Nathan tipped his hat again and began strolling away from her.

Maddy snickered behind him, calling, "Thanks again, deputy."

Turning his head a little, Nathan nodded once to acknowledge her, but he kept walking. He heard the thud of a closing door and knew she'd returned to her shop. Nathan sighed deeply as he shook his head.

Geez, why do people always try to set others up?

While Nathan occasionally wondered what kind of person

he could finally fall for, he'd never met anyone who made him wish for something permanent.

Maybe someday.

Until then, Nathan was content to head into the city every few months to find someone to scratch his itch with.

Nathan was passing behind *Spiron's Bar and Grill* when movement in the trees to the right caught his attention. Moving closer, he peered between the thick pine foliage. Nathan lifted his brows when he spotted someone straightening from where he stood partially behind a tree.

"Malcolm?" Nathan called, recognizing the shirtless young man. "Malcolm Louvre?"

Malcolm spun, revealing the surprise etched on his features. "Uh, h-hello, deputy." He quickly fastened the fly of his jeans as a blush stained his tanned cheeks. "Um." Bending, Malcolm reached into a duffle at his feet and pulled out a shirt. He was clearly at a loss for words.

Taking in Malcolm's half-nude form and untied shoes, Nathan frowned as unease filled him. "Uh, Malcolm, what are you doing?"

Twisting his shirt in his hands for a second, Malcolm cleared his throat. "Um." He seemed to catch himself, for he shook out the fabric, revealing a nice polo shirt. "My car's in the shop, so I figured I'd just, uh, jog to work," Malcolm told him before tugging on the shirt.

Nathan crossed his arms over his chest as he arched a brow at the young man. "That doesn't explain your state of dress, Malcolm. You were almost at a point where I could write you a ticket for indecent exposure." While Nathan wouldn't do it, the man who worked as a cook at *Spiron's* needed to give him a little better explanation.

Malcolm gulped audibly, his eyes growing wide. "Please don't do that, sir," he cried. "I didn't think anyone would see me change back here." Shoving a hand through his thick black hair, Malcolm continued, "I didn't want to be all sweaty at work. The kitchen's hot enough as it is, so I brought clean clothes in my duffle bag." He waved a hand toward the bag he'd pulled the shirt from. "That way they'd be clean."

Nathan could see the tense lines in Malcolm's neck and the way his attention flickered past him toward the restaurant. Nibbling his bottom lip, he shifted from foot to foot. Nathan could easily see that Malcolm was hiding something.

More is going on here.

Over the last few years, Nathan had seen his fair share of *oddities* around Stone Ridge . . . and in the forest. Things he couldn't really explain and had never talked to anyone about and never planned to. Many of the people there were secretive. They would rather handle things themselves instead of involving the law. On many occasions, Nathan felt certain they went to the park rangers as opposed to the police.

Considering how douchy the prior sheriff was, Nathan could understand the sentiment. He'd noticed that attitude had begun to change, slowly, now that there were new faces in office. Sheriff Anthony had hired a few new people, since a couple had expressed their desire to retire.

Nathan couldn't imagine the department without Markus, Grady, or Lyle, but all three intended to leave soon. Markus already had his last day set for the end of the month. Grady and Lyle would probably be with them for another year, giving Anthony plenty of time to settle in and find their replacements.

When Malcolm shifted his weight once more, Nathan realized the young man was still waiting.

Blowing out a breath, Nathan rested his hands on his hips. "Well, I guess I didn't actually *see* you naked, now did I?" he drawled with a smirk. Seeing Malcolm duck his head, he chuckled. "Use the restaurant's restroom next time, Malcolm," he ordered with a shake of his head. "No nudity in town. Got it?"

"Yes, sir," Malcolm immediately replied while nodding.

Nathan patted Malcolm on the shoulder before turning away. Hearing the roar of more than a couple of motorcycles, he headed toward the front of the restaurant. While he knew the youngster was hiding something, there wasn't anything he could do about it.

Besides, just as Nathan had told him, he hadn't actually *seen* him nude.

Arriving at the street, Nathan took in the sight before him. There were nearly a dozen motorcycles just parking at the restaurant. He spotted a couple more with trailers continuing up the Main Street leading out of town and deeper into the forest.

"Damn," Nathan murmured, admiring the large assortment of motorcycles. "Nice collection."

Nathan saw a couple of the motorcycles had sidecars, and a smile teased his lips at the sight. One of those sidecars contained a big dog with a helmet and goggle set on its head. He found himself taking a couple of steps toward the group, wanting a closer look at the bikes, before he caught himself.

"All right, Khan." After removing his own helmet, the big brown-haired man who'd been driving that motorcycle leaned over and eased the headgear off the dog's head. "Let's see what this place has that'll interest you. Hmmm?"

The dog woofed softly, then jumped from the sidecar. It paused and shook out its light gray fur. Then it began walking beside a couple of the other riders toward the bar.

That was when it hit Nathan. The animal that he'd at first thought was a sort of German shepherd hybrid, was in fact, a wolf. While Nathan didn't think Russell—the restaurant's owner—had a hard policy against pets in the bar, as long as they were well-behaved, Nathan wondered what he would think about a wolf.

Wait. Wolves require special permits to own.

Realizing Nathan had to verify that they owned the animal legally—Khan, the big man had called him—he started toward the group. "Excuse me," he called.

The big man with the wolf turned to face him. As the guy swept his attention over Nathan, the scar over his left cheek pulled oddly as he offered him a slight smile. He even dipped his chin in a slight nod.

"Deputy," the man greeted, his voice deep. Lifting his hands in placation, he added, "I know we look a little rough, but we won't cause any trouble."

Nathan smiled and rested his hands on his hips. "Didn't think you would," he assured the guy. "I'm Deputy Nathan." Waving a hand toward the wolf, he stated, "And I need to ask you about your wolf."

"This is Khan. Had him since he was a pup," the guy claimed. He rested his hand on Khan's furred head. "He's perfectly safe."

A guy with pale skin and red hair scoffed and rolled his eyes. The black-haired man standing beside him whapped him on the stomach with the back of his hand. The redhead immediately slung his arm around that guy's waist and kissed his temple.

The big scarred man sighed. "Really." He seemed to be trying to reassure Nathan. "Khan is fine."

Suddenly, Khan stepped forward, his nose sniffing deeply.

Nathan instinctively took a step back while lifting his hands away from his body when the big animal nuzzled his hip. The wolf whined softly while moving his nose to Nathan's stomach. Finally, it licked at Nathan's hand before slipping his head under his fingers as if asking to be pet.

"Huh." The brown-haired man crossed his arms over his chest as his eyes narrowed speculatively. "Looks like he really likes you."

"That's, uh . . . nice," Nathan commented, feeling uncertain. He gave in to the wolf's request and lightly rubbed his ears. "Uh, I was just asking because they require special permits to own," he told the man. "Do you have them with you?"

The man arched a brow, his surprise evident. "Uh, not on me, no," the man began. He turned and looked at another man. "Hey, Draven. Do you have the permits for our having Khan?"

A slender man with pale-blond hair stepped forward. His blue eyes peered intently at Nathan. "Of course," he stated.

Just when Nathan was certain he caught a flash of red in the man's eyes, Khan turned and growled. He planted his butt on Nathan's foot, his back to him, and pinned his ears back. Draven took a step back and glanced at the scarred man.

"Uh, I just remembered. Kontra has them, Sam." Draven peered at the scarred man—Sam. "He's with the sheriff. Maybe we should call him?"

"Good plan," Sam replied, pulling a phone from his pocket. "I'll give him a quick call."

Nathan felt the hairs on his nape stand on end. He wasn't entirely certain what actually would have happened if Khan hadn't growled, but he felt certain it would have been one of those *oddities* that he saw around town.

What the hell is going on?

CHAPTER TWO

Khan had never wanted to shift so badly. His mate was standing right next to him, and he couldn't talk to him. Instead, he was in wolf form and could do little but nuzzle his hip.

Until Draven had approached.

Knowing that Beta Sam hoped Draven would implant the memory of him showing Nathan bogus documents, Khan had done the only thing he could. He'd planted himself in front of his mate and growled. As odd as the thought was, Khan didn't want any other being to rove around inside his mate's head.

To Khan's relief, Draven had caught on quickly and backed off. Instead, the others were scrambling with a way to fulfill the deputy's request without messing with his mind.

"Sam?" Kontra's deep voice came through the line questioningly. "Something wrong?"

"Not *wrong*," Sam told their alpha. "Just unexpected."

"You know I stopped to talk to Sheriff Anthony Holsteen, so I'm assuming it can't wait," Kontra stated, his tone filling with concern. "What's up?"

"Are you with the sheriff now, Al, uh, Kontra?" Sam asked.

"I am," Kontra confirmed.

"Well, we've run into one of his deputies." Sam glanced at Draven before returning his attention to the deputy in question. "He's asking about our permits to own our wolf, Khan, and Draven reminded me that you had them." His eyes narrowed just a little, and the faintest tick showed at the corner of his jaw. "Since you're with the sheriff, you mind if I put you on speaker?"

Kontra hesitated in responding. It was only due to his shifter hearing that Khan heard the man mutter, obviously to the sheriff, "How many humans on staff?"

"Just one," a tenor voice replied. "Deputy Nathan Kaldwell, and as far as I know, he's not aware."

A second later, Kontra's voice sounded louder. "You're on speaker, Sam," he told him. "You sure Draven didn't have them?"

Khan knew what Kontra was really asking.

Why didn't Draven neutralize the problem?

Unable to help himself, Khan growled low in his throat. Recalling who was on the other end of the line, he cut off the noise with a whine. Khan offered a few low woofs to add to his displeasure.

"Is that Khan?" Kontra's surprise came through clearly in his tone.

"It is, Kontra," Draven responded, telling Khan that, at some point, Sam had put Kontra on speaker, too. "He's taken a shine to the deputy." Humor entered the vampire-warlock's tone. "Although, I think the deputy is a little uncertain what to think of that."

"Deputy Nathan?" The tenor voice was louder. "Are you with Kontra's men?"

"Yes, sheriff," Nathan responded. "I was admiring their motorcycles, gorgeous collection, by the way, when I realized Khan wasn't a dog, but a wolf."

"Thanks," Sam replied with a grin upon hearing the compliment. "We have a couple of mechanics in the group who keep them in tip-top shape."

Nathan tipped his head in acknowledgment before continuing. "Anyway, I recalled that owning wolves required a permit, and when I asked, there seemed to be some confusion on the matter."

"Ah, okay," Sheriff Holsteen stated. "Well, Kontra did bring some paperwork with him." He stated the lie smoothly. "Let me take a quick look to see that everything is in order."

Nathan's brows furrowed, and his scent took on just a bit of disbelief. Obviously, his mate was astute. Of course, he would have to be for him to do his job effectively.

"Yup. Have no fear, Deputy Nathan. The guys are good to have their wolf." Sheriff Holsteen's voice sounded warm through the line even as a rustle of papers could be heard, too. Khan wondered if the man had grabbed some random pieces of paper and shook them just to make it sound good. Then the sheriff added, "I appreciate you coming in to see me, Kontra, and letting me know you and your guys would be in the area." With a chuckle, he added, "It'll make it easier to alleviate the townsfolk's fears, just in case anyone asks." Sheriff Holsteen sounded resigned when he said, "I have a motorcycle myself and enjoy riding it often. Used to do a lot of traveling, and I know the stigma others can paint us with."

Is he rambling just to make Nathan feel better?

"People can feel that way about us," Kontra rumbled in agreement. "Especially when it's a group my size."

"I'm sure I'll see you around," Sheriff Holsteen claimed. "Maybe I'll even take a ride with you." A little louder, he asked, "You good now, Deputy Nathan?"

"I'm good, sheriff," Nathan responded, although his scent told a different story. "I appreciate the confirmation."

"Certainly." Khan thought that would be it, but the sheriff wasn't done. "You know, my deputy enjoys motorcycle rides, too. He's been here all his life, so if you want to know about anything, Nathan can direct you."

"Thank you," Kontra responded. "Sam, we good?"

"Yes, sir," Sam replied, his gaze still on Nathan. "Thank you, sir. See you soon." Then he disconnected the call and shoved his phone into his pocket. With a small smile, he dipped his chin in a nod. "Sorry for the confusion, Deputy

Nathan."

Deputy Nathan nodded slowly, his gaze falling back to Khan. "So, uh, you gonna give me back my foot, Khan?"

To Khan's pleasure, Nathan scratched his ears some more. Tingles of heat and need spread from where his mate touched him, and for the first time in Khan's life, he had to fight back getting a boner in wolf form. Then he processed what Nathan had actually asked him.

Khan's butt was still firmly, protectively, planted on Nathan's foot.

Peering up at Nathan, Khan took in Nathan's amused smile. He couldn't help himself. Seeing that smile, he tucked his nose into Nathan's groin and snuffled, relishing his mate's intense, masculine scent.

Gods, but my human smells good.

Even as Khan heard Payson snicker, Nathan muttered, "Okay, okay. That's a little too friendly," as he pushed at Khan's head.

As much as Khan didn't want to, he gave in to Nathan's urging and put a little distance between them.

"So, Khan," Sam rumbled, gaining his attention. A small smirk curled the side of his mouth, while Khan heard Payson snicker again, and even Draven let out a quiet chuckle. "Your mate, I take it?"

Khan rumbled softly in the back of his throat as he dipped his muzzle in a nod.

Sam hummed, eyeing Nathan speculatively. "All right." With a cock of his head, he stated, "So, you ride, huh?"

Nathan was giving Khan an odd look, but at Sam's question, he focused on the big shifter. "I do," he confirmed. "Got a *Harley Street Glide* at home."

"Nice," Draven cut in. "You'll have to come out and ride with us some time. You can show us some nice windy roads around here."

Nodding slowly, Nathan commented, "Kontra said you

were staying in the area for a while?"

Sam jerked a small nod. "We're meeting up with Declan and his husband, Lark." With a roll of one large shoulder, he admitted, "Our doc is collaborating on a . . . side project with Lark." Sam smiled as he glanced toward the diner where most of the gang who'd stopped had entered. "And Ishmael, he's one of our guys, has a brother who lives around here, too, so they're gonna catch up."

"You have a mechanic and a doctor in your group?" Nathan sounded surprised.

"Yep. We're semi-nomadic, so a number of the guys are skilled in different areas to keep us all safe and healthy," Draven told him, glancing toward Vail, who'd exited the bar and was heading their way. "Got a few bases here and there." As soon as his beloved was close enough, Draven slipped his arm around the other wolf shifter's waist and drew him close. "We're not sure how long we'll be here, but Declan told us about a large farm house out his way that we could rent."

"Food's ordered," Vail murmured, tipping his head and pressing a kiss to Draven's clean-shaven jaw. "Got you a bacon cheeseburger."

"Mmmm, thanks, love," Draven responded, turning his head and pecking a kiss to his lips. "Sounds perfect."

Nathan chuckled. "Oh, anything you get from Russell's bar is always good." Shoving his hands into his pockets, he told them, "I'm partial to their brick-oven pizza, myself."

Vail grinned at him. "A few of those were ordered, too."

"You won't be disappointed." Then Nathan turned his attention back to Sam. "Well, I'd best be getting back to my patrol." He took another step back. "Sorry for interrupting." Tipping his chin toward their collection of motorcycles, Nathan added, "You really do have a nice assembly of bikes."

Khan barely managed to suppress his whine of dismay when Nathan began turning away.

"Deputy Nathan, wait." Sam had obviously noticed Khan's distress. "What's your number, man?" He pulled his phone back out. "We're serious about riding with you."

Payson waggled his reddish-brown brows as he teased, "And your boss did offer your assistance in showin' us the sights."

Nathan squinted at Payson for a second before focusing on Sam. "Here." He held out his hand for Sam's phone.

Sam woke the device before relinquishing it. After pressing more than a few buttons, the soft chime of a device in Nathan's pocket rang through the air. Nathan returned Sam's phone.

"Now you have my cell, and I have yours." With a tip of his hat, Nathan began to turn again. "Nice to meet you, Sam." Then he smirked and focused on him. "Khan."

Khan desperately wanted to head after his mate, but he knew it was a futile gesture. He couldn't keep in his quiet and appreciative whine. His deputy cut a fine figure in his uniform shirt, form-fitting jeans that hugged his ass just right, and cowboy boots.

"Easy, Khan," Sam rumbled softly, threading his fingers in Khan's ruff—the hold was soothing as well as probably intended to stop him if he took off after Nathan. "We'll help you secure your mate."

"Yup." Payson came forward with Land tucked tight against his side. "Your pretty deputy won't know what hit'em."

Just as Khan growled at Payson—the hyena shifter should not be commenting about his mate—Land once again whopped Payson's abdominals with the back of his hand.

"No checking out other guys," Land grumbled, frowning at him.

Payson barked a laugh as he turned to face Land, wrapping his second arm around him. "Not checkin'im out, my mate," he claimed, completely ignoring Khan's growl. "Just statin' a fact. Khan's deputy is pretty." Then Payson lowered his head and began nibbling on Land's neck as he growled, "But no one holds a candle to you, babe."

Land moaned softly, tipping his head to the side and offering Payson more room.

"Ease off, Payson," Sam ordered gruffly. "Don't wanna scare the locals." As Payson cackled and lifted his head, Sam focused on Khan. "And as much as I never want to say *Payson's right*, in this case, he is. We'll help you." Ignoring Payson's renewed laughter, Sam pinned Khan with a surprisingly kind smile. "Maybe now you'll be able to shift."

Khan didn't bother to try to respond. He would correct their misconception soon enough. As much as he didn't want to give up the safety of his furry form, Khan knew that, for his mate, he would—at least, some of the time.

"Come on, Khan," Sam encouraged, releasing his grip on his scruff now that Nathan was out of sight. "Let's see what Ryan's ordered for us."

Turning away from where Nathan had disappeared, Khan fell into step beside Sam. He hoped the guys were right.

For the first time in years, Khan felt a mixture of hope and excitement.

I met my mate.

CHAPTER THREE

To Nathan's surprise, he received a call from Sam the very next morning, inviting him to ride with them . . . again. As tempted as he was, he wasn't certain joining them was the best idea. Nathan knew something odd had happened on that sidewalk the day before — one of those *oddities* that happened around town.

Nathan didn't know if being alone with the bikers was a good, or even safe, idea.

Fortunately, Nathan had once again been able to use work as a way to put someone off. He was on his third day of rotating ten-hour shifts. Until Sheriff Anthony hired a couple more people, just about everyone's schedules were a little wonky.

Although the days flew by with few incidents.

Just as Nathan had predicted, he'd ended up running into Maddy's granddaughter, Cindy, while getting a morning cup of coffee at *Miss Martha's Muffins*. The woman was a pretty blonde with just a little extra padding around her midsection. In Nathan's mind, it didn't detract from Cindy's beauty, but he felt zero response from his body. To that end, when Cindy had asked him out, Nathan had carefully declined.

Although Cindy had seemed disappointed, Nathan had been able to make his escape when the barista called his name with his coffee.

Nathan hurried out of the shop and began his morning patrol. When noon approached, he returned to the station. He spotted the sheriff manning the desk and offered his boss a smile and nod.

As Nathan passed, he stated, "I'm on lunch for the next hour, sheriff. Then I'll be back to take over the phones from you."

"Sounds good," Sheriff Anthony replied, relaxing in the chair. The man opened his mouth, then closed it again just as quickly.

Hesitating, Nathan wondered if the man needed something. When the sheriff turned his attention back to the computer, he decided he must have been mistaken. Nathan headed to the breakroom and the sandwich and fruit salad he'd left there for himself that morning.

After eating, Nathan took over the phones. He knew the two hours he would be manning them would finish out his shift. Personally, he appreciated it when that happened as it gave him plenty of time to write up any needed reports.

The afternoon was predictably quiet, with only one call about someone returning home to find their front door open to break up the monotony. Nathan had radioed for Deputy Nereo to driver over there. The newly hired male had been the one on patrol, and he'd called back that the door had been left open by the woman's son, who had shown up unexpectedly. Everything had been fine.

Better safe than sorry.

Just as Markus arrived to take over for the next stint on the phones, Sheriff Anthony walked out of his office. He stopped beside the desk and greeted Markus. Then Anthony turned and focused on Nathan.

"I have a favor to ask," Anthony stated, surprising Nathan. "I need you to run out to this address and do a wellness check on the occupant." He glanced at the piece of paper he held in his hand before focusing on Nathan again. "A Misses Clair Waldorf. I guess she lives out there alone, and her daughter, who lives in Denver, hasn't been able to reach her the last few days."

"Clair Waldorf?" Nathan took the paper, looking at it to

confirm the information. He couldn't think of anyone with that last name living near Stone Ridge, but he supposed he didn't know everyone, regardless of the fact that he'd lived there all his life. "Uh, shouldn't Deputy Goliath go?" Nathan hated to second-guess the sheriff, but perhaps he'd forgotten that Nathan was off shift and the other deputy was currently the one out on patrol. "I'm just about to go off shift."

"I know you are, deputy." Sheriff Anthony's smile appeared a little strained. "But that address is in your neck of the woods, isn't it?" As Nathan glanced at it again to read it — *yep, it sure is, so why don't I know this woman* — Anthony added, "And I need Deputy Goliath to head in another direction."

Markus glanced up from where he'd taken over the chair, a look of surprised disbelief on his face. He even opened his mouth as if to question Anthony. When the sheriff narrowed his eyes just a smidge, Markus snapped his mouth shut and returned his attention to the computer.

Yep. Oddities.

Still, Nathan couldn't refuse his boss, no matter how strange he thought the request was. "Yes, sheriff," he responded dutifully. "I'll take a look."

"Thanks." Sheriff Anthony clapped him on the upper back once before turning and heading back toward his office. "Enjoy your day off tomorrow, Nathan."

Nathan chuckled as he started toward the break room and his jacket. "Yeah, I'll really love all the cleaning, laundry, and grocery shopping I need to do."

Sheriff Anthony chuckled. "Yep, it adds up."

After getting his things, Nathan headed back out the front, noticing Markus now stood in the doorway to the sheriff's office. He was speaking to the man in low tones, but Nathan could still make out the dark-haired deputy's murmured question of, "Why are you sending Nathan out there?"

As much as Nathan would have liked to have heard the answer, whatever Anthony said caused the other deputy to enter the office and close the door behind him.

Huh.

Nathan zipped his jacket against the weather and headed outside. Inhaling deeply, he enjoyed the crisp fall air. Halloween was fast approaching, and he admired the festive decorations springing up in all the shop windows as he headed to the side lot where he'd parked his pick-up.

After climbing behind the wheel, Nathan clipped the note with the address to his dash. His older model vehicle didn't have GPS. Nathan had been asked by his older sister's husband on a couple of occasions why he hadn't replaced it, yet, but to Nathan's way of thinking, if it wasn't broke, why fix it. His old truck still got him from point A to point B safely, so why change?

The engine fired right up, and Nathan started on his way. Truth be told, the address was a ways past his turn-off for his own road. A light smattering of snow decorated the sides of the road, and he wondered if the motorcycle riders were actually going to stick around. Winter in Colorado really wasn't conducive to their mode of transportation.

Winding a bit further up the mountain, Nathan finally found the address. The gravel road was nicely graded, and the trees had obviously been trimmed recently. He pulled up to a large farmhouse tucked in a large clearing. There was a large detached shop to the left with its doors closed.

Nathan stopped and panned his gaze over the place. Everything appeared quiet. He did see smoke coming from both of the farmhouse's chimneys, so he knew someone was inside.

Maybe Clair's phone died or something.

Ready to have his task taken care of, Nathan quickly texted Markus that he was at the house and was heading up to knock on the door. It was always a good policy to let another officer know where he was. Especially when on police business.

Markus quickly texted back with a *thumbs up* emoji.

Nathan snorted under his breath.

Definitely not *the standard police response.*

Climbing the couple of stairs leading to the large front porch, Nathan took in the number of rockers on it. Some were singles and some were doubles. In all, he saw eight chairs with a couple of old cable spools turned on their ends to be used as tables. One even had a large checker board drawn on it, and the checkers themselves were stacked around the base.

Just who is this woman?

Nathan lifted his hand in a fist and knocked loudly. If he didn't get a response within a minute or two, he would knock again, shouting that he was the police. After that, Nathan would have to round the home trying to find some way inside.

He really hoped it didn't come to that.

To Nathan's relief, it didn't. After only a few seconds, he saw the flutter of the curtain in the window to the left of the door. Nathan suddenly felt grateful he was still in uniform, since that would most likely ease a little old lady's fears if she really did live out here alone.

Am I making assumptions about her being a little old lady? Hmmm.

Nathan heard the snick of a lock disengaging a few seconds later. His relief at spotting the signs of life were short-lived. A little old lady didn't answer the door. In fact, it wasn't a woman at all.

"Sam," Nathan murmured, frowning. "What are you doing here?" Just as quickly, another thought hit him. "Are you squatting at Misses Waldorf's?" Moving his hand to the butt of his service weapon, Nathan demanded, "Where is she?"

After a quick glance toward Nathan's weapon, Sam slowly lifted his hands, palms out. "There's no Misses Waldorf here," he told him. "I'm sorry for the subterfuge, Nathan." While Sam kept his deep voice soft and low as if trying to soothe him, it didn't work when his next words were, "You refused to meet up with us, so we had to think up another way to get you out here."

"Subterfuge?" Nathan took another step backward, wariness surging through him. "Why?"

"Khan wants to meet you," Sam told him, confusing him further. "Officially, I mean."

"Your wolf?" Nathan shook his head even as he frowned at the bizarre man. "You wanted me to come out here to see your wolf?"

Sam chuckled quietly, mirth filling his brown eyes. "Not quite what I mean."

"Invite the man in, Sam," a deep voice from deeper in the house ordered. "We have plenty to discuss, and you're letting in the cold."

"Yeah, it's Colorado in the fall, man." Nathan recognized that voice as the teasing redhead from the diner. "If Land and I were fuckin' in the front room, you'd have frozen our dicks off by now."

Sam scowled even as he took a step backward and peered to the right. "Why the hell would you be fuckin' in the front room, Payson?"

"Eh. Maybe the mood struck, and this was where we happened to be," Payson responded glibly. "It could happen."

"No fucking in the front room unless you're alone in the house, Payson," the first deep voice ordered with a hint of long-suffering in his tone. "You know we don't want to see it, and you don't *really* want us to see it, either."

Letting out a chortle, Payson responded, "Yes, boss."

Another man appeared at Sam's shoulder, and Nathan stared up at the guy. He was even bigger than Sam, and that was saying something because Sam stood six-foot-four and was built like a brick outhouse. This guy also had a larger presence, which screamed *guy in charge*. His thick salt and pepper hair and goatee, as well as his intense brown eyes, gave him a slightly unnerving look, and Nathan sure as hell wouldn't want to meet him in a dark alley.

"I'm Kontra Belikov," the man told him, holding out his huge paw of a hand. "And we needed to talk to you, Nathan, so Anthony helped us out."

That was when it hit Nathan. "He set me up?"

"He did," Kontra confirmed, clearly unrepentant, still holding out his hand. "Come in."

"Why?" Nathan asked incredulously, even as he hesitantly reached to take the intimidating man's hand.

Except, when Kontra shook, he didn't try to squeeze or dominate. He kept his grip comfortable, and Nathan found himself appreciating the warmth of the guy's palm. The man was right, after all. It was growing colder by the minute now that the sun had set.

"Come inside, Nathan," Kontra encouraged, tugging lightly with his hold. "And we'll explain everything."

Nathan wondered if he had much of a choice. As he started moving forward, he wasn't certain if they would allow him to leave unless he obeyed. Nathan must not have hidden his trepidation well enough, for Kontra offered him an encouraging smile.

"Try to relax, deputy," Kontra urged, releasing his hand once Nathan stood in the foyer. "You're perfectly safe here. This really isn't a bad thing."

"It's really not," a soft voice piped up from off to the right. When Nathan looked into the sitting room, he spotted the slender black-haired man sitting on Payson's lap, and he was smiling widely at him. *That must be Land.* "It's really actually a totally cool and special thing." Then the guy tipped his head to the side a little as he added, "Of course, at first, you'll probably find it a little odd. I know I did."

Payson began pressing kisses down Land's neck and over his shoulder as he mumbled against his flesh, "But I made it worth it, didn't I, baby?"

Land tipped his head to the side and answered in a breathy voice, "Yes. Oh, yes, you did."

Kontra sighed even as he beckoned Nathan forward. "Come on into the great room. It'll be more comfortable." The huge male began leading the way down the center hallway. "Can we get you something to drink?"

"No, thank you," Nathan replied with a glance behind him. At some point, Sam had closed the front door, blocking out the cold. "Uh, so, what's this all about?"

Even while asking the question, something Land had said niggled in his brain. The guy had found whatever a little odd. *Oddities.*

Nathan wasn't certain he wanted to know, and he really didn't understand why these guys would suddenly decide to tell a complete stranger about their business.

"Let's start with the basics," Sam told him, falling into step beside him. "We're not a cult, and we're not doing anything illegal."

A muscular, dirty-blond-haired male scoffed as he started down a staircase to the left of the hall. "Well, most of the time."

"Ryan," Sam scolded gently as he lifted a hand to welcome the other man. "That's not illegal. That's stopping those doing illegal shit."

With a wide grin, Ryan stepped close, accepting Sam's embrace. "Right. Blowing up the facilities isn't illegal. My mistake." As he spoke, he wrapped his own arm around Sam's waist and peered up at him with mischief in his hazel eyes.

"Exactly," Sam replied without missing a beat. Then he lowered his head and kissed the other man.

Ooookay. A lot of couples around here.

Nathan looked down the hall and saw a patiently waiting Kontra. Moving past the pair, he figured he should just get it over with. "You blow shit up?" Nathan questioned. "If you think I can get you explosives or something, I'd never do that."

Kontra shook his head, a smirk teasing the corners of his lips. "We make our own, if it comes to that," he claimed, not discounting Ryan's claims in the least. "No, this is about something else." Heading through an arch to the right, Kontra led the way into a large living room where one of the fireplaces roared happily. "Anthony said you're perceptive, and he thinks you already have an inkling about what I'm going to share with you."

With a grimace, Nathan rubbed the back of his neck, trying to ease the tension building there. He decided he'd just better get it out there. "Please tell me you're not intending to use your wolf to hunt the werewolves in our woods."

Yeah, I know there's paranormal shit around here.

Nathan had just never discussed it with anyone. They'd never hurt anyone, and he respected the right to privacy.

Kontra's dark brows shot up, his surprise obvious. A second later, he barked a laugh as he shook his head. "Nope. Definitely not that."

"Well, then what?" Nathan demanded, not certain he believed the big man.

Continuing to grin at him, Kontra claimed, "Khan is one of those werewolves." His dark eyes twinkled as he added, "Although we call ourselves shifters, and we're not restricted to wolves." Kontra rested his hands on his hips, eyeing him. "Oh, Fate gives us a soul mate that we recognize by scent, and Khan recognized you as his mate."

Shifter. Fate. Mate.

Nathan swallowed hard. He'd heard many men who he'd suspected of hiding *oddities* call their partner mate. He'd always thought it a term of endearment.

Could it be more?

What would it mean to me?

Sucking in a sharp breath, Nathan whispered, "I'll have that drink now."

CHAPTER FOUR

K han lay on the floor of the kitchen in the cabin deep in the woods, watching as Ishmael met his older brother again for the first time. Both wolf shifters had been held captive and experimented on by scientists. While Kontra and his people had rescued Ishmael, Alpha Declan's people had rescued Boaz.

The brothers had been taken to different facilities, which meant what had been done to them had varied. Both testings had started out trying to create a larger, more aggressive wolf shifter that they could dominate and control. The assumption was that the scientists wanted to use them to track down and help capture more shifters for testing. As Boaz's tests had progressed, whatever they'd done to him had caused him to go nearly feral, losing himself in his wolf. Boaz was supposed to have been put down, but Declan's people had saved him before that could happen.

Unfortunately, it had been too late to reverse the testing, leaving Boaz trapped as a huge aggressive wolf. Boaz had been kept in this remote cabin while Declan's people had tried to figure out how to reverse what was done. Only Boaz meeting his mate in a large, dominant sungazer lizard shifter named Adisa had pulled Boaz out of his aggression . . . which the wolf still struggled with.

For that reason, Adisa and Boaz sat together on a sofa on the far side of the room. Adisa kept his arm around Boaz's shoulders while Boaz sat with his hands clasped on his thighs. Boaz smiled tightly at Ishmael even as he seemed to vibrate with barely restrained nerves.

Everyone else stayed near the kitchen area.

"It's good to see you, Ishmael," Boaz rumbled quietly. His deep voice and massive body were at odds with his surprisingly nice-looking boy-next-door looks. "I'm glad to see you're safe." Boaz's attention slipped to the man sitting beside Ishmael—his brown bear shifter, Madagascar. "And I'm really happy for you that you've found your mate. Congratulations."

"Thank you, Boaz," Ishmael replied, smiling widely as he glanced Madagascar's way. "Mads has made my whole life better." His expression sobered as he refocused on Boaz. "I'm sorry I don't remember, uh, you or, well—" Ishmael paused, stumbling over his words. "Um, was our pack happy, uh, before?"

"It's okay, Ish. I understand. I didn't know anything or anyone for a long time." Boaz rubbed over his thighs before moving one hand to Adisa's thigh. "I'd never wish that on you, so maybe . . . maybe what happened to you was better in the long run."

When Boaz's tests had rendered him feral, Ishmael's testing had been put on hold. Doctor Meyer—the female scientist who'd been working on Ishmael—hadn't wanted her project to go to waste while she figured out what had gone wrong with Boaz. She'd wiped Ishmael's memory, and through punishments and medication, she'd made him think he had hallucinations about wolves if he didn't stay on the meds.

Ishmael hadn't known anything about his shifter heritage until Madagascar had stumbled upon him acting as a janitor at Doctor Meyer's facility. That place was no longer there. Kontra's people had blown it sky-high.

All things considered, Khan was sort of relieved that he'd been sold to and held by witches instead of scientists. They occasionally drew his blood to be used in their spells, but for the most part, he was left alone. The worst part was being trapped in a cage to be ogled by tourists.

"And, yeah," Boaz continued with another small smile. "Our pack was a happy one to grow up in before we were attacked." His expression turned vacant with a hint of fondness. "Our parents were fated mates, and they loved us all very much."

"All?" Ishmael cocked his head. "Who all?"

"We had an older brother. Cain," Boaz revealed, pain filling his black eyes. "He was killed during the raid." With a soft scoff, Boaz murmured, "Cain was a good brother. Took his oldest brother responsibilities very seriously. He helped Dad teach us to shift, then worked with both of us."

For the next thirty minutes, Khan listened with half an ear as Boaz shared many happy memories with Ishmael. He was tempted to get up and leave the cabin. There was a large doggie door installed in the wall under a window, but Khan didn't want to draw attention to himself.

Khan figured he probably shouldn't have come, but he and Ishmael had become friendly — at least, while in wolf form. He loved playing with the other shifter. Ishmael had been altered to become a massive black wolf, too, but he hadn't undergone the aggressiveness chemicals that had messed with Boaz. Ishmael was as big and friendly as a wolf or man.

Besides, Khan had needed something to do to keep his mind off of Nathan. His mate hadn't accepted any of Sam's invitations to join them on a motorcycle ride. Kontra had told Khan that he was going to try another tactic, but he hadn't told him what it was. That was probably because Khan still hadn't revealed that he could shift.

Maybe they would confide in me or ask my opinion if I could actually talk back.

With that thought in mind, Khan decided that when he returned to the farmhouse, he would reveal his ability. Then maybe someone could take him into town. Khan could pretend to run into Nathan.

Yeah, maybe I should have thought about doing that before.

Khan just hated the idea of spending so much time out of his fur.

Come on, man. Channel your inner Khan.

Barely biting back a chuff of amusement at his thoughts, Khan refocused on the conversation going on around him. He noticed movement from some of the others. A couple of Alpha Declan's people had accompanied Khan, Madagascar, and Ishmael, showing them where the cabin was, but Khan didn't recall their names. Madagascar's brother, Congo, and his mate, Zhaul, had joined them for support, too.

Everyone but Adisa and Boaz were rising and moving toward the door. They stayed seated, waiting.

Finding his paws, Khan began doing the same. Most everyone had already filed out by the time he reached the open door. Madagascar and Ishmael were bringing up the rear.

"Ish?" Boaz called.

Pausing, Ishmael turned back with his ready smile in place. "Yeah?"

Boaz sucked in a big breath. He clenched and released his hands once, twice. Then Boaz crossed the room and wrapped his arms around Ishmael.

"It's so good to see you, brother," Boaz whispered, but it was loud enough for Khan's shifter hearing to make out. Boaz continued, "I can't go into town, yet. I'm not ready, but don't be a stranger, okay?"

Ishmael hugged Boaz back. "I won't," he promised. "I'll be back."

Boaz jerked a nod before releasing Ishmael. He quickly rushed back to the other side of the room where Adisa wrapped him in his arms. Burying his face in Adisa's neck, Boaz seemed to shudder, as if letting out some emotion or maybe getting himself back under control.

After a few seconds, Madagascar wrapped his arm around Ishmael's waist and guided him out the door.

Khan followed. A glance back showed Adisa rubbing Boaz's back with one hand while cradling his nape with the other. Khan wondered what it would feel like to have Nathan comforting him that way.

"So, now you know where the cabin is," the sandy-haired wolf shifter commented as he led the way to the quads they'd used to reach it. "Just be sure to call and make certain Adisa is here before coming. Otherwise . . .

The guy trailed off his words, his implication clear. Adisa tempered Boaz's aggression. If Adisa wasn't there to do that, there could be trouble. Adisa had been an enforcer for the Shifter Council for decades, but when he'd found his mate in Boaz, he'd resigned. That didn't mean they didn't occasionally call on Adisa to do something for them, as long as it wouldn't take him too far from his mate or for very long.

"We hear ya, Nick," Madagascar replied with a nod. He held out his free hand to the wolf shifter. "Thanks for bringin' us up here."

"Happy to." Nick—the wolf shifter—shook Madagascar's hand. "Miach and I come up here to visit when we can." Nick rested his hand on the odd-smelling human's back. "The interaction is good for Boaz, and he really is a great guy when he's in control."

Once again, the implication was clear—Boaz wasn't always in control.

Khan wondered briefly what he did when he lost control. Then again, maybe he didn't want to know. He certainly never wanted to see Ishmael hurt by his own brother.

Yeah, that's a horrible thought.

"Hey, Khan," Congo called, getting his attention. "You runnin'? Or do you want to ride on the quad?" The bear shifter pointed at the padding attached to the rear rack of one of the quads.

After a second of hesitation, Khan decided to ride. He was the only one in animal form. They'd taken it fairly easy on the way up when Nick had shown them how to get there, so he hadn't had any trouble keeping up. However, with his new plan in mind, Khan wanted to get back to the farmhouse as swiftly as possible.

Khan easily vaulted onto the padded area. Spreading his paws, he braced them on the metal railings of the rack.

Congo climbed on the machine. Others did the same to several more. Zhaul had his own while the other mated couples shared.

With a pat on Khan's flank, Congo told him, "I'll be careful, but bark if you're uncomfortable."

Khan rumbled softly in response, indicating that he'd heard. Then he endured his first quad ride. He didn't find it particularly enjoyable, but he figured if he were in human form, it might have been different.

As soon as they arrived at the parking area, Khan was more than happy to jump down. He paused and stretched his legs, arching his back with his tail in the air. Then he shook himself before making his way to the large SUV they'd all arrived in.

Nick and Miach had picked them up at the farmhouse.

Lying between the middle captain's chairs, Khan made himself comfortable for the ride back.

Upon reaching the farmhouse, Nick parked beside a pickup that Khan didn't recognize. The second he exited the SUV, however, he knew who it belonged to. His mate's scent hung faintly in the air.

Excitement rushed through him, and Khan bounded eagerly to the door. He yipped, prancing in place, trying to hurry the others along. They'd paused to talk to Nick and Miach some more about the possibility of shifter hunters being in the area.

Hunters. Gods.

Just the thought chilled Khan to his bones, and he didn't

want to think about them. Instead, he wanted to think about his mate.

Upon seeing his antics, Congo headed toward him.

"Everything okay, Khan?" Congo questioned, climbing the steps.

Khan did his best to roll his eyes even as he sniffed before turning his muzzle to the door. He rumbled softly as he refocused on Congo.

The bear frowned at him, but at least he opened the door.

Bolting inside, Khan followed Nathan's fresh masculine scent. He quickly located his mate in the large living room. Khan skidded to a stop and practically vibrated with excitement.

Finally, my mate is here.

Khan barely resisted shifting that instant. He had just enough presence of mind to scan who was there and take in the scene. After all, Khan didn't think Nathan knew about shifters, and he didn't want to freak out his mate.

Nathan was still in uniform, and he sat in a chair with a tumbler of amber liquid cradled between his hands. His brown brows were drawn together, and a muscle ticked in his jaw. Lines of tension tightened his shoulders and limbs, and his scent had definitely taken on a stressful note.

Nathan was definitely upset about something.

Kontra sat with his mate, Tim, on one small sofa, both looking concerned. "Like Land said," Kontra was saying. "It's not a bad thing. Besides, you already knew there were paranormal things out there."

"That didn't prepare me for being paired up with a random stranger," Nathan countered, scowling at Kontra.

"He won't be a stranger once you get to know him," Sam stated from the larger sofa where he sat with Ryan.

Are they talking about me?

Scowling at Sam, Nathan stated, "But you said he's stuck in his wolf form right now." He rubbed the back of his neck as he straightened in his chair. "How can I get to know him like that? And do you have any idea how long he'll be trapped in that form?"

Yup. They're talking about me.

"Ah, so this is why Khan was so excited." Congo's deep voice came from behind him, drawing attention to them both. The brown bear shifter chuckled softly. "Good to see you finally turned up, Nathan."

Nathan's focus fell on Khan, and he stared at him with an inscrutable expression for one heartbeat, two. After downing the rest of his drink, he set the tumbler aside. He licked his lips as he rubbed his palms over his thighs.

"So, Kontra said you understand while in wolf form, Khan," Nathan stated, staring at him. "And you recognized something in my scent that makes you think I'm your mate."

Evidently, the others had already done a lot of explaining.

When Nathan continued to stare at him, Khan realized his mate expected some type of reaction. He dipped his chin in a nod.

"And you can't shift right now," Nathan continued slowly, seeming to still be wrapping his brain around the information he'd been given. "But under normal circumstances, were-wolves, or shifters, rather, can change at will."

Right. I need words. I need my human form.

Crouching, Khan blew out a slow breath as he closed his eyes. He reached for his human form. Khan knew he wasn't fast, but he could shift, and he needed to prove it.

CHAPTER FIVE

Nathan gaped as the wolf he knew as Khan began to change shape right there in front of him. Sure, Kontra and the others had claimed it happened, but as the saying went, seeing was believing.

Fur seemed to sink into the wolf's skin. His body rippled and contorted. The sound of muscles popping, bones creaking, and tendons snapping filled the room. The noise set Nathan's teeth on edge, and his mouth was suddenly so dry he wanted another bourbon.

Then Nathan's mouth felt dry for a whole new reason.

Ten feet in front of Nathan knelt the prettiest man he'd ever seen in his life. Expressive pale gray eyes met Nathan's own through the fall of messy, tawny-colored hair. The lean, toned man nibbled his bottom lip before swallowing hard enough that his Adam's apple bobbed.

A surge of desire to taste those lips, to nibble that Adam's apple, rushed through Nathan faster and harder than he'd ever felt anything in his life. He would trickle sipping kisses down his long neck and across his torso. Nathan wanted to suckle the pretty little nipples on display before traveling down the lean lines of his abdominals to the treasure trail that led to his naked prick.

Wait. Naked.

Jumping to his feet, Nathan surged forward. He swiftly began stripping his coat from his shoulders.

The move must have startled the pretty man, for he jerked backward, falling on his butt.

Nathan felt horrible when he spotted the fear filling his gray eyes. "Shit, sorry," he muttered, holding out his jacket. "Didn't mean to"—Nathan crouched and began wrapping the fabric around the naked man—"startle you."

"I-It's okay." The man's voice came out a soft tenor that did funny things to Nathan's stomach. He accepted Nathan's jacket, sliding his arms into the sleeves. "Thank you."

"You're welcome." Nathan hesitated, not yet wanting to pull away. With his hands still on the slender male's shoulders, he asked, "Can I help you up?"

"Hmmm," Kontra mused. "I'm guessing that's not your first shift since we rescued you." He arched one dark brow questioningly. "Something you want to tell us, Khan?"

"Khan shifted?" Payson hollered before rushing into the room. The guy had either already been heading their way, or he'd been eavesdropping. Sliding to a stop a few feet away, Payson grinned broadly at them. "About damn time." Then the redhead cocked his head and smirked at him. "And already wearing your mate's clothes. Damn, man. You work fast." Payson finished by giving him two thumbs up.

Frowning, Nathan slid an arm around Khan's shoulders as he helped him to his feet. "He was nude in the middle of a room full of people," he stated defensively as he led him over to a free sofa. "Of course, I offered him my jacket."

Fortunately, said jacket, which fit Nathan's larger, broader frame, was a bit large on Khan. It fell to the tops of the other man's thighs. When Nathan helped to seat him on the sofa, he quickly grabbed the throw blanket from off the back and wrapped that around him, too, before taking a seat beside him.

Glancing around the room, Nathan noticed a number of amused expressions on the other men's faces. "What?"

Why the hell are they all looking at me like that?

"That right there, is the mate-pull in action, Nathan." Kontra offered him a warm smile as he pointed at them. "Your automatic, instinctive need to care for Khan."

"He was nude in a room full of people," Nathan reiterated, frowning at them all. "You all shouldn't be ogling him."

Kontra chuckled. "No one but you, you mean."

Nathan glared at the big man. "No one without permission."

Nathan didn't mention that he'd wanted to do more than just ogle the man. How could he not? The man he still hadn't released was absolutely stunning. Plus, he cuddled into Nathan's side, fitting there absolutely perfectly.

And why am I cuddling him? Aren't these his friends?

Peering down at the gorgeous man, Nathan found him peering at him through his lashes. His confusion and ire at the others faded as he stared into his pretty gray eyes. Nathan felt his heart speed up in his chest, and heat flooded his veins. Having this man in his arms felt so damn perfect, and his instinct said to keep him there.

But why?

Mate-pull.

Nathan's heart began to speed up in his chest for a new reason as confusion and disbelief began to flood him.

But that's just crazy. I don't even know him.

"So, can I get you a refill, Nathan?" Ryan asked as he rose to his feet. "I figure you're gonna need it soon." Then he smiled at the man Nathan held. "And what about you, Khan?" Then Ryan narrowed his eyes as he cocked his head. "Is there another name you'd like to be called by?"

"And why didn't you tell us you'd started shifting?" Tim asked bluntly. "I mean, from the fairly easy change, Kontra has to be right." He waved in the general direction of where Khan had been on the floor. "That can't have been your first time since we rescued you."

"You can keep calling me Khan. I sorta like the name. And you're right. It wasn't my first time shifting," Khan admitted. After worrying his lower lip for a few seconds, he told them,

"But it's so much safer staying in my fur. I have teeth and claws, and my four paws can run me to safety so much faster than two feet." Huddling even closer to Nathan, Khan whispered, "Being in human form is dangerous and scary."

Concern for a new reason flooded Nathan. He rubbed his hand up and down Khan's opposite arm, attempting to soothe him. "Being human is scary?" Nathan questioned. "What're you afraid of, baby?"

Damn. Where the hell did that endearment come from?

Nathan couldn't recall calling anyone anything like that in his life.

Okay. Maybe this mate-pull thing is real after all.

What the hell am I going to do now?

Even as Nathan waited for Khan's response, he knew he would have a lot of thinking to do when he got home. Except, home meant letting go of the man in his arms. Nathan knew he shouldn't have trouble doing that, but damn did he not like thinking about letting go.

Good grief.

"Hunters," Khan answered simply. "There always seem to be someone hunting us."

"There's no hunting in these national forests, Khan," Nathan stated, doing his best to reassure him. "Regardless of what form you're in around here, you'll be safe." Khan stared up at him, disbelief in his expression, so Nathan added, "I don't know how big the wolf shifter pack ruling this area is, but surely they wouldn't allow hunters around them."

That made sense to him, anyway.

Congo sighed deeply from where he leaned against the wall with his arms crossed. "Actually, we learned from Nick today that there could be a hunter presence in the area." With a grimace, he added, "He said the current standing order for their pack was to never run alone and always make certain someone knows where they'll be."

"What?" Nathan scowled at the big male. "There's hunters

here? Have you notified the park rangers?"

Kontra snorted, smirking at him. "Where do you think we get our information from, Nathan?" He pointed toward the woods out the window. "The head park ranger, Declan McIntire, is the alpha of the wolf pack in this area." Scoffing, Kontra added, "Hell, I got his permission to be here before bringing my guys into the area." He shrugged one big shoulder, adding, "Politics."

Nathan accepted the refilled glass of bourbon from Ryan and drank half of it in one go. As much as the rest tempted him, he paused and rested the tumbler on his thigh. He frowned at the rug-covered floor beneath his booted feet and shook his head.

"I'm sorry we're turning your world upside down," Khan whispered. "If I could've spared you, I would have." After taking the bottle of water that Ryan offered him, he used his other hand to rub over Nathan's chest. "I was just as surprised as you when I smelled you outside the pub and acted on instinct."

Jerking his attention to Khan, Nathan asked, "You would have walked away from your mate?" He glanced between Kontra and Sam and saw that both sported disbelieving expressions. Nathan returned his attention back to Khan just in time to see him shrug one shoulder as he blushed. Shaking his head, Nathan murmured, "I don't think I believe you."

Khan nibbled his bottom lip for a second before whispering, "You deserve so much better than me."

Before Nathan could think up a response—after all, he didn't know the man—Khan jumped to his feet, pulling away from him. Even as he reached to draw him back to the sofa, the shifter skittered away while shedding his jacket. Seeing Khan start to shift, Nathan called the male's name.

Khan's change from man to wolf was far faster than the reverse, and Nathan sat too long in stunned silence.

Soon enough, Khan was racing from the room. The wolf ignored not only Nathan calling him, but Kontra and Sam, too. He disappeared down a hall and out of sight.

Blowing out a harsh breath, Kontra waved toward where he went. "Payson, please follow him." The big male shook his head as he muttered, "He shouldn't be out there alone."

Payson appeared both troubled and confused. "I'll get Vail, too." After a quick kiss to Land's lips, he started out of the room, adding, "He's good at getting people to talk."

"You mind if I go, too, Mads?" another man asked. The guy was big and broad, and sported a troubled expression.

"Of course, you can go after your friend, Ish," the slightly smaller but no less broad goateed man who was holding Ish rumbled. "Just be careful, my mate."

Ish nodded. "I will." After the pair kissed, the larger one hurried after Payson.

"That was not the way I'd hoped for this to go," Kontra grumbled, scrubbing his fingers through his hair, betraying his frustration. He arched a brow as he turned to Tim and asked, "You saw nothing about any of this?"

"Afraid not," Tim replied, drawing his brows together with worry. "I mean, I know I'm not the only one that often scents fear from Khan." He glanced around, and Nathan saw several of the other men nodding as if confirming Tim's comment about smelling fear from Khan. "I thought bringing his mate to Khan would help settle him."

"Khan smells afraid?" Nathan questioned, glancing around the group. "What's that mean?"

Ryan returned to his seat and settled beside Sam once more. "We told you that shifters have heightened senses."

Nathan nodded. "I recall."

He could see pros and cons to that, considering some of the smells out there in the world.

"Well, emotions give off certain scents," Kontra explained

41

before taking a sip of his own drink. "Like anger, fear, happiness, even arousal and lies." Tapping the side of his nose, the big male claimed, "Normally, we're trained to figure them out after our first shift. We can tell a lot by how someone smells."

Nathan remained silent, only giving a tiny nod of acknowledgment. He didn't know what to say to that.

Well, shit. They can smell arousal and lies? That has to make things tough at times.

"We don't know what Khan's running from," Kontra admitted, looking frustrated. "He hid that he could shift, never talked to us, and we know nothing about his past."

Groaning, Sam added, "Hell, he says to call him Khan, which obviously isn't his real name." He frowned as he stared down the hallway where the men had disappeared. "Payson picked it out for him."

"Could his real name be attached to trouble?" Nathan tossed the idea out there. "Are there wanted shifters?"

Lifting his hands, palms up, displaying his confusion, Tim stated, "We have a Shifter Council, and they have lists of known rogues. If Khan's on it, I can't imagine why." Scoffing softly, Tim mused, "There's not a mean bone in that skittish wolf's body."

"If someone listed Khan as rogue, then it was by someone trying to cover up their own crime," Kontra stated with conviction. "But we won't know unless he tells us."

"It's a moot point, Kontra," Sam countered, frowning and shaking his head. "He's with us now. He's part of our pack. Has our protection." Waving a hand, he added, "Hell, if he bonds with Nathan here, then he'll end up with the protection of Alpha Declan and the Stone Ridge pack, too. He just needs to stop running."

Nathan downed the rest of his drink and rose to his feet. Grabbing his hat from the nearby end table, he placed it on his head. Then he grabbed his jacket from the floor and started toward the door.

"Where are you going?" Sam demanded as they all rose.

Looking over his shoulder at them, Nathan paused only long enough to tell them, "If Khan wants me, he knows where to find me."

"You're his mate," Tim declared, scowling at him. "Don't you want to help him?"

Nathan turned and sighed. "Sure I do, and not just because of the whole mate thing." Although that definitely ramped up the need. Resting his hands on his hips, Nathan declared, "It's obvious that young man was abused, but if he won't talk to any of us, all we can do is be there for him when he's ready to change his mind."

"Then why are you walking away?" Kontra demanded quietly.

"I'm not," Nathan assured. "I'm doing what I can to secure Khan's safety." Before they could ask another question, he told them, "I'm going to talk to the people who know about these hunters in the area and make it safe here for Khan."

With that declaration, Nathan headed out of the house.

CHAPTER SIX

Khan's wolf howled mournfully as he forced his animal to run away from their mate. His animal didn't understand why they'd left the human. He wanted to turn right around and go back to the living room.

Instead, Khan kept them moving down the hall and out the side doggie door. The chilly evening air wrapped around them, and he'd never felt so grateful for his fur. Khan needed a run to clear his head.

As his feet tore up the light dusting of snow that had managed to fall to the ground between the pines, Khan couldn't suppress his whine. He'd never been at odds with his wolf before, and he struggled with his warring instincts. Part of him desperately wanted to go back to his mate, but his fear kept him running.

Khan didn't deserve such a fine mate, a wonderful human who'd seemed ready to accept him just like that. His mate didn't know him. He didn't know about his past or the reason why he'd ended up a witch's plaything. If Khan ever explained how his own shifter pack bought their freedom with his worthless hide, he felt certain Nathan would turn away from him.

It's better this way.

This way my mate can't reject me.

With that thought in mind, Khan ran ... and ran. He leaped over downed branches, ducked under low-hanging ones, and pushed through the brush. Khan had no particular destination in mind. His one goal was to tire his wolf.

Slowing at the edge of a clearing, Khan peered around the forest, trying to get his bearings. Except, he'd only been in the area for a few days. He'd certainly never run so far before.

Khan had no idea where he was. A look at the sky showed him the moon had traveled quite a distance, so he'd been running for hours. His tired limbs told him the same thing. Huffing, Khan sat on his butt as he realized he really only had one choice.

He would need to turn around and follow his scent trail back the way he came. Well, he supposed there was another option. He could wait for someone to find him.

Except, what if it was a stranger from the wolf pack that located him? Would he get into trouble?

And what must Nathan be thinking of me?

Growling to himself, Khan wondered how he could be so stupid. Earlier that day, leaving the cabin, he'd been prepared to shift and ask Kontra to help him manage going into town. Then the alpha had surprised him by having Nathan in his home, damn near ready to accept him, and he'd let his fears and insecurities get the better of him.

Except, earlier at the cabin, Khan hadn't known about the hunters in the woods. They'd discussed that on the drive back to the farmhouse. Scenting Nathan there had driven the information out of his mind until Congo had brought it up again.

And Kontra had already known! When had the alpha planned to tell the rest of them? What if Khan had gone wandering by himself and unwittingly gotten captured?

Oh, you mean what we're doing right now? Running away from our mate and wandering alone in the woods?

Khan mentally groaned upon hearing his wolf's angry snarky comment in his mind. Still, he couldn't exactly counter his animal. The wolf was right.

The snap of a twig behind Khan had him up and spinning. He sidled to the left, keeping to the shadows. Going backward would leave him exposed in the clearing. Instead, Khan hid under several low-hanging pine bows.

A second later, Payson's hyena's nose shoved under those same branches. The enforcer stared at him for several heartbeats before pulling back again. The hyena's normally playful, teasing visage was nowhere in sight. Instead, he looked annoyed.

Cringing, Khan eased out from under the branches. By the time he'd exited, Payson was already in human form. He stood with his fists on his hips and his feet braced while frowning down at him.

On either side of Payson sat Vail and Ishmael. The pair of wolves appeared a little more sympathetic, eyeing him with concern. Once Khan was out from under the wet pines, they even came forward and rubbed against him — one on each side — covering him with their scents and reminding him that he was pack — that he wasn't alone.

Khan sighed, relief filling him. Then he focused on Payson, ready to face the music.

"Shift," Payson snapped, frowning intently at him.

For a few seconds, Khan tried to resist the command. Payson wasn't the alpha, after all. Unfortunately, the hyena shifter was pretty damn dominant in his own right, even though he usually hid it beneath snark and inappropriate comments, and Khan's wolf had always been extremely submissive.

Which was why his pack had been happy to get rid of him.

As soon as Khan shifted, he rested on his knees on the ground and wrapped his arms around his torso, trying to keep in as much body heat as possible. He appreciated that his two friends pressed against him. Their fur was a little on the damp side, but the body heat still seeped through.

"Good grief, man," Payson snarled. "You make us chase you all the way out here? What the fuck for?" He growled as he frowned at Khan. "And don't forget about lyin' by omission to our alpha or leavin' your mate. Stupid, man." Shaking his head, Payson curled his lip in a sneer as he continued, "And do you know what the worst part is? Do ya?"

There was a worst part?

"N-No, sir," Khan managed to whisper because it seemed like Payson's attitude demanded it.

His voice rising, Payson declared, "The worst part is that I could be curled up with Land in a nice warm bed, but instead, I'm out here freezin' my balls, chasing your dumbass all over the mountainside." With a huff, he crossed his arms over his chest and asked, "Where were you going and why?"

Khan opened his mouth, then closed it just as quickly. His mind remained stubbornly blank. He had no answer to that.

"Really? Nothin'?" Payson rolled his eyes. "Typical." Pointing at him, he stated, "Here's what we're gonna do. We'll shift back, and you're gonna follow us home like a good doggie."

While Khan wanted to feel offended, he couldn't dredge up enough dignity to do so. "Yes, sir," he mumbled.

"Then, when we get back," Payson continued as if he hadn't spoken. "You're gonna march your ass inside. If your mate's inside, you'll apologize. If not, you'll at least explain to Alpha Kontra what the hell your problem is that you decided to go racing out into gods-middle of nowhere like a douche."

Khan had never seen Payson angry before, and he hung his head with a wince, shame filling him. "O-Okay, sir." He feared the hyena shifter would step forward and backhand him at any minute.

For several long seconds, nothing happened, and he stayed where he was, tense and waiting.

"Oh, for fuck's sake," Payson muttered with a whine in his voice. To Khan's surprise, the other shifter dropped to his knees in front of him and drew him into a fierce hug. In a much softer voice, Payson asked, "What the fuck in our time together ever gave you the impression that I used my fists on my pack-mates?" As Payson spoke, he kept Khan tight against him with one hand while threading the fingers of his second through Khan's hair. "We all got issues, man, but you may wanna think about talkin' to the pack shrink about yours."

Khan stiffened at the idea of going to someone like that, and Payson obviously felt it. He eased back a little, using his hold in Khan's hair to force him to look him in the eyes. The anger in their depths had been banked to be replaced by serious concern—which was sort of disconcerting, considering who was holding him.

"Khan, or whoever the fuck you are," Payson stated with way too much seriousness in his voice. "There's nothing wrong with talking to someone about your problems. If you can't go to Alpha Kontra about it, then find someone." With a shrug, he added, "I was experimented on, and I needed to talk to someone about it. Now I don't know what happened with the witches or if your issues were prior to that, but you need to talk to someone who can help you figure out a way to let at least some of them go." Payson held his gaze steady for several heartbeats before he added, "Ya hear me?"

"Y-Yeah," Khan managed to get out. "I-I'll th-think about it." That was the best he could manage.

Payson's eyes narrowed, and his nostrils flared. A tick appeared in the corner of his jaw. For an instant, Khan thought Payson would push.

Except, fortunately, he didn't.

Dipping his chin in a short, sharp nod, Payson huffed a breath. "Okay then." He released him and began turning away. As he moved, Payson smacked Khan's ass cheek with a resounding crack. "I'm tired of freezin' my dick off, so let's get out of here."

Then Payson shifted, and Khan followed suit.

As it turned out, Khan had been running a fairly circuitous route. They weren't that far from the farmhouse as straight shots went. The home's welcoming lights appeared between the trees after only a twenty-minute run.

Someone must have been watching for them because the back door opened when they were halfway across the back clearing. Alpha Kontra stood silhouetted in the doorway for a few seconds before he took a few steps backward. He stayed quiet as they passed, closing the door behind them and blocking out the chilly evening air.

While the other three immediately began to shift, Khan hesitated.

Once Payson was in human form, he blew a raspberry at Khan. "Cats outta the bag, man." He narrowed his eyes just a smidge before saying, "Do as I ordered."

Khan's wolf immediately backed down, and he shifted.

As Khan finished, Kontra murmured, "You were gone longer than I thought you'd be, guys."

Payson scoffed as he rolled his eyes, his happy-go-lucky persona back. "Khan's wolf is a speedy fucker." Land entering the room had the hyena shifter turning toward his mate. "Hi, baby." Opening his arms, he welcomed the human between them. "Missed you."

Then they were making out.

Vail rolled his eyes before grabbing several sets of sweats out of a cabinet by the door. "He could have at least covered before starting that shit," he commented as he handed a pair to both Khan and Ishmael before pulling on a set himself. "We better leave, or we'll end up with an eyeful we don't want."

"Hot drinks are set up in the kitchen," Kontra told them, lifting a hand to herd them in that direction. "Let's go."

They all quickly started moving. Evidently, the only one who wanted to see Payson's erection was Land.

As it should be. I wonder what our mate's erection looks like. Bet it tastes good.

Khan mentally groaned at the ideas his wolf was putting in his head. Just thinking about an aroused Nathan caused his own blood to heat. Unable to help himself, the words were out before he could censure himself. "Is Nathan still here?"

"No, Khan. He's not," Kontra replied calmly. "But I don't think you expected him to be."

Sighing, Khan shook his head. "No, I suppose not."

"So, we have coffee, cocoa, and hot toddies." Kontra pointed at the offered drinks. "Help yourself."

Khan hesitated. He'd lost the taste for coffee while in captivity. But if he were to get through any type of question and answer or explanation with Kontra, he wanted the comfort of a hot drink. Khan also knew it would warm him up fast.

"Um, are the hot toddies in here?" Khan asked, pointing at the lid-covered pot that had a dipping spoon beside it.

"They are," Kontra confirmed.

"I'm all for that," Vail stated with a grin. He squeezed Khan's shoulder in reassurance. "I'll get the mugs."

While they chose that, Ishmael went with a hot cocoa with a dash of mint-flavored Irish cream in it. When they filed into the living room, the others were met with their mates. They offered hugs and kisses of welcome.

After Ishmael softly asked Khan if he was going to be all right and received his assurance, Madagascar wished everyone a good evening and took him up to bed.

Kontra turned to Khan and swept an assessing gaze over him. "Did you want to talk about any or all of what happened tonight, Khan?" The big grizzly shifter kept his voice low and soothing.

"Not really," Khan admitted. As Kontra nodded, still staring at him, Khan got the impression that the alpha would have let the matter drop. Except, Khan had given his word to Payson, and afraid little wolf or not, he still kept his word. "But I told Payson I would try."

Nodding once more, Kontra rumbled, "Okay."

Vail scoffed softly, his smile turning wry. "Yeah. We saw Payson all serious and shit." Blinking wide eyes, he added, "It was seriously messed up."

"That would have been something to see," Draven claimed with a twist of his lips.

Kontra remained focused on Khan. "Would you like to sit here before the fire?" He indicated the warm and comfortable seating. "Or would you prefer the seclusion of the front den?"

Khan hesitated, glancing at the others. Movement to his left told him Sam and Mutegi had arrived. Payson also leaned against the wall, now wearing sweats and a very satisfied, relaxed expression.

Huh. That didn't take him long.

What would it be like to get a quickie from my mate anytime I wanted?

Bowing his head, Khan knew that to have any chance to experience anything like that with Nathan, he needed to do this.

And I only want to do this once.

Indicating the seating before the fire, Khan murmured, "Here is fine."

Khan knew that by choosing the great room, he was silently saying that anyone from the inner circle was welcome. Evidently, others had been listening in the wings. Several other pack members entered, drinks in hand, and everyone made themselves comfortable.

Sitting as close to the hearth as possible, needing the heat to keep a chill from settling in his bones, Khan decided where to begin.

"I was the youngest child of my parents. I have an older brother and sister," Khan told the others haltingly. "In my birth pack, weakness was not an option. You were strong or it was beaten into you." He heard a couple of swiftly indrawn breaths, but he didn't look up from his drink to see who it was. Instead, Khan continued, "I learned two valuable lessons. How to hide that I'm not dominant in any way, shape, or form, and how to run from a situation when I knew I'd be found out."

Lifting his gaze, Khan focused on Kontra. "It worked until my alpha made a deal with the witches, and I was the payment."

CHAPTER SEVEN

Nathan had always known where Declan McIntire lived, but he'd never had cause to go there before. He'd talked to him on the phone several times, though, and met him in passing while working together. As Nathan parked before the house, he wondered what the wolf shifter would do with him turning up at his doorstep at —

Geez, is it already ten-fifteen at night?

Damn.

Unwilling to back out, Nathan climbed out of his truck. He hesitated, then removed his service weapon and locked it in the glove box. Then he took off his utility belt, rolled it up, and placed it on the floorboard.

As Nathan headed toward the door, he mentally shook his head at himself. He still couldn't believe he'd ended up drinking in uniform. He mentally winced at the *faux pas*, but it was too late to change it.

Hopefully, the liquor on my breath isn't too bad.

Nathan hesitated a few seconds, then knocked on the front door. Shoving his hands into his pockets, he waited . . . and waited. He pulled out a hand, preparing to knock again when he heard it — the unmistakable sound of feet moving along hardwood.

Taking a step away from the door, Nathan felt his heartrate kick up a notch. He heard the locks disengage and mentally winced. Whoever it was should really have checked before opening the door so late at night.

When the door swung open, Nathan tipped his head up to

meet the gaze of the alpha wolf of the Stone Ridge pack. He felt another uptick of his heartbeat as well as the hairs on his neck standing on end. Nathan finally understood why staring into the man's dark-gray eyes always felt just a little disconcerting — as if he were looking into the eyes of a predator.

And now it makes sense.

The corners of Declan's lips quirked up. "Deputy Nathan Kaldwell, to what do I owe the pleasure?"

Nathan felt the distinct impression that Declan already knew, but he answered honestly anyway. "I apologize for calling on you so late, but I need to talk to you about the hunters."

"The hunters?" Declan arched one black brow. The African American's lightly Irish-accented voice took on a slightly amused hint. "What hunters are ye referring to, Deputy Nathan? These are protected lands."

Is he really going to play dumb with me?

"Please, call me Nathan," he countered. "And we both know what hunters I'm talking about." When Declan just narrowed his deep gray eyes at him, he stated bluntly, "The wolf shifter Khan is my mate, and he's running scared of hunters your people told him about. I need to fix this."

Declan's eyes widened at that. His nostrils flared as he took a deep breath, telling Nathan he was scenting him. After his talks with Kontra, why some people around town appeared to be smelling others made sense.

The knowledge also gave Nathan a pretty good idea of who he knew that were shifters and who might not be.

And there are a lot of them.

Taking a step backward, Declan beckoned. "Ye'd best come in, Nathan. This could take a bit."

Nathan entered Declan's home and took a cursory look around. The large place held a little bit of a lodge-like feel. There was plenty of open space to the right, and he could see all the way back. A huge great room with a TV hanging over the fireplace was to the right with an open-concept dining room and kitchen beyond. The wall on the left led to a hallway, and open stairs leading upward faced the back of the house.

"Who was at the door, hon?" a tenor voice asked as a petite blond man appeared from the hallway. "Oh. Hey, deputy." The blond's brows furrowed. "Everything okay?" Then he rolled his eyes as he shook his head. "Of course, it's not. You're here late at night. Should I start some coffee?"

Nathan knew the little cutie was Doctor Lark Trystan. He'd once worked at Sugar Creek Memorial but had since opened his own practice. Everyone called the man Declan's husband, although Nathan couldn't recall a ceremony. Considering the man's five-foot-five stature, he also wondered if he was a wolf shifter, too, or something else.

"I don't think so, my mate," Declan replied, crossing to Lark. "Maybe some finger sandwiches, though." Resting one hand on his lover's waist, Declan threaded the fingers of his other through Lark's blond hair. "Nathan's here on pack business, and we'll probably need the food to soak up the alcohol." With a tsking noise, he looked over his shoulder at Nathan. "Especially since he's already been in the bourbon."

Nathan winced and moved his gaze to the wall.

"Pack business?" Lark murmured, his blue eyes widening. "I didn't realize he . . ." His voice trailed off as he blinked a couple of times. "Uh, yeah. Okay."

"We'll be in me study, Lark," Declan told him before pecking a kiss to his lips. "See you in a minute."

"Come on, Nathan." Declan beckoned with a couple of crooked fingers. "Let's get comfortable."

Following Declan down the hallway, Nathan joined him in the first room on the left. A large study with a good-sized seating area on one side opened before him. Declan headed to the sideboard and picked up a decanter.

"More bourbon?" Declan asked, grabbing a tumbler. "This could take a bit to explain."

"Uh, I probably shouldn't." Nathan rubbed the back of his neck as he glanced at his uniform shirt. "I really shouldn't have before, but—"

"Eh, at least ye're not armed," Declan said teasingly, and a fresh wave of embarrassment flooded Nathan. Pausing, Declan's eyes widened as he stared at him. Then he barked a laugh. "Ye were before, weren't ye?"

Nathan let out a huff before grumbling, "To be fair, Sheriff Anthony tricked me into going to Kontra's farmhouse." He crossed his arms over his chest as he admitted, "I *thought* I was going there in an official capacity."

"And they ambushed ye with the news that paranormals are real, and ye're the mate of one," Declan hazarded astutely. When Nathan nodded, he chuckled again. Then he waved the tumbler he'd filled toward Nathan's chest. "So, take off the uniform shirt and drape it over a chair if ye're that self-conscious."

Nathan only hesitated a second before quickly doing just that, leaving him in his white wife-beater. Declan was there holding out his glass, and he took it. After a grateful sip, Nathan ran his hand through his hair, wondering what else to say.

"So, the assholes hunting shifters. I'll explain what we've been going through," Declan began, crossing back to the sideboard. As he poured himself something from a different decanter, he commented, "If ye were introduced to paranormals and Khan as yer mate this evening, I'm a little surprised to see ye here, though." Then Declan waved toward the furniture. "Have a seat."

With a sigh, Nathan settled into a thickly padded leather chair. He frowned at nothing as he took another drink. Then he refocused on Declan.

"Like I said, Khan is running scared," Nathan said with a shake of his head. "I know he wants me, and I'll not deny I want him, but he ran away when Congo and Kontra started talking about hunters." Cocking his head, Nathan squinted at the far wall as he mused, "Something in his past messed him up, but Kontra and his guys don't have a clue. Hell, until this evening, they hadn't even realized he'd regained the ability to shift. Khan had hidden it from them."

Declan hummed. "That does sound like a wolf not used to sharing." With a smile, he added, "It also sounds like a wolf who's trying to protect you, even if only subconsciously."

"How do you mean?" Nathan focused on Declan, curious if the wolf would have any insights.

"Well, a shifter's first instinct to his mate is to make certain he's safe," Declan explained, expanding on the basics Kontra and Sam had shared that evening. "After that, it's healthy, happy, and well-cared for." With a smirk and a suggestive eyebrow waggle that did not at all fit the big black male, Declan added, "Well-cared for in *all* ways."

"Have you been hanging around Prier too much, Declan?" Lark teased as he entered the room carrying a tray laden with finger sandwiches, as well as a couple of types of chips, dip, and salsa. The blond smirked at his lover. "Talking about sex already?"

Declan grimaced. Sounding contrite, he muttered, "He does rub off on people, doesn't he?"

"Who's Prier?" Nathan asked instinctively. As a cop, he was always looking for more information.

Lark set the tray on the coffee table before heading toward the sideboard. "Prier is a pack member mated to our head enforcer." After opening the right-side cupboard to reveal plates, he said with a roll of his eyes, "He always has sex on the brain." Lark grabbed several, and his expression turned speculative as he returned. "I think it's because he's making up for lost time."

"Still?" Declan asked incredulously. "After being mated to Kajika for over a decade?"

With a shrug, Lark asked, "Do you have a better explanation?"

Declan scoffed. "He says shit just to get a rise out of people. No other reason."

Lark laughed. "Yeah. I can see that." He waved at the plate and food. "Help yourself."

"Thanks." Nathan set his tumbler on a side table and leaned forward, doing just that. He'd skipped supper, after all. "So, you were saying." Nathan glanced Declan's way before turning his attention to the food. "Khan may be trying to unconsciously protect me?"

While helping himself to his own food, Declan nodded. "Probably. And if he has such a troubled past as ye think, he probably doesn't even realize he's doing it." With a plate of food balanced on one knee and Lark cuddled up to his other side, Declan appeared comfortable and relaxed. "If he thinks hunters are going to come after them, he wouldn't want to draw attention to the fact that ye're mates. Then ye'd be in their crosshairs, too."

"I'm a deputy." Nathan couldn't help but feel a little offended. "I *can* handle myself."

Lark scoffed, grabbing one of the sandwiches off of Declan's plate. "That won't mean shit to a shifter. No offense." He shrugged. "It's hardwired into their DNA."

Declan nodded. "Khan could be the most submissive shifter ever born, and he would still try to protect his mate." He shrugged. "That's just the way it is. Especially since ye're human." Lifting his free hand, Declan added, "Again, no offense."

"What you really need to do is pin him down and get him to bond with you," Lark stated with a firm nod. "Remind him of the fact that after you're bonded, you get some natural enhancements."

Nathan nodded slowly as he chewed his bite of chicken salad sandwich. While he wasn't normally a big fan, he had to admit, Lark's were pretty good. He would happily eat a few of them.

"Kontra mentioned something about that, but we covered a lot of information." Nathan racked his brain for what the big man had told him. "Uh, faster healing and metabolism. Higher resistance to disease. Slightly stronger and better senses."

"Exactly." Declan pointed the rim of his tumbler at him. "Just remember, there are cons, too. Yer aging will slow to match his, so ye'll outlive family, if ye have any." He furrowed his brows as he added, "Those humans close to ye would notice yer lack of aging, so ye'd eventually have to fake yer death and hide out until they'd no longer remember ye."

"You can only go to certain doctors, too," Lark cut in, raising his hand. "Like me. Someone who isn't going to freak out about any possible blood anomalies."

Even as Nathan continued to nod, his mind returned to Declan's comment. He could very well outlive his older sister . . . by a lot . . . as well as his niece and nephew. They would eventually think he'd died.

"Damn," Nathan muttered absently. "That sucks."

"At least there are several of us around," Lark stated, looking concerned. "And we have the ability to cover up a problem if you do end up at the wrong hospital."

After swallowing his sip of bourbon, Nathan shook his head. "No, I mean the pretending to die to your friends and family." He grimaced, admitting, "I'm close with my sister and her family."

"I'm sorry." Declan sighed. "I said there were cons."

"But you'll always have a faithful lover by your side," Lark pointed out softly. "And you have your pack. You wouldn't be going through that alone."

Nathan nodded. Then he blinked and refocused on the pair cuddled up on the sofa. He felt a small kernel of jealousy take root in his gut. They were obviously a well-fitted pair with their shit together. Nathan wanted that.

And I have to get Khan on board to get it.

"Well, to have that problem, I still need to convince Khan to give me a chance," Nathan reminded them. "And I think that means figuring out this hunter shit." Waving his hand absently, which held a chip, he nearly caused the French onion dip to fly off of it. Fortunately, he caught it in time. "Okay. So. What have you and your people been dealing with that you've been keeping from the police?"

Declan chuckled as a feral smile curved his lips. "Ye know, *you* are the last human at the sheriff's office." His grin widened. "I'm gonna like having a staff that's all paranormal or those in the know. It's going to make things so much easier around Stone Ridge."

"They're all shifters there?" Nathan asked curiously.

"Except Nereo," Declan told him. "He's a vampire."

"Oh." Nathan nodded. "Of course he is."

Over the course of the next hour, Nathan ate, drank, and listened to Declan explain what had truly been going on behind the scenes in the Stone Ridge and Colin City area. Events included private and government-funded science experiments, CIA interference, military experiments, and rogues bent on revenge after getting kicked out of the territory. The last in the long list had been bigoted fanaticism about the number of homosexuals in the area, accidently drawing shifter hunters to them.

Nathan fell asleep on Declan's couch, his mind reeling with information until it had no choice but to shut down.

CHAPTER EIGHT

Once again, Khan climbed into Beta Sam's sidecar. This time, however, he was in human form. The jeans, boots, and jacket felt restrictive after so many years in wolf form.

Khan knew they were required to fit into the human world, so he sucked it up.

After sliding the helmet on his head, Khan buckled his safety belt. He rested his hands on his thighs and clenched them into fists. When he felt the shiver work through the motorcycle when Sam brought it to life, Khan fought back a tremble of his own.

He wasn't certain this was the right course of action, but he knew he needed to explain things to his mate. He needed to make it right with him. Maybe, if he did that, his human would be willing to wait until it was safer for him to be bonded with a shifter.

Khan knew that Konta and Sam had Nathan's phone number, and it had been so very tempting to just call him. His need to look into his human's eyes, as he explained, had won out. He needed to see Nathan's response and take in his scent to be sure.

To that end, Sam was driving him to Nathan's house. They'd received the information from Sheriff Anthony. Accompanying them—because they never went anywhere alone, a testament to how dangerous the area had become—was Sam's mate, Ryan, on his own motorcycle. Hunter, a human, and his penguin shifter mate, Yuma, were with them, too.

Evidently, the pair were really good at calming people.

Khan sort of wondered if they'd been sent to keep an eye on him, not Nathan.

Oh well.

As they started rolling, Khan gripped the edge of the sidecar. He watched the trees zip by and tried to quiet his mind. Khan knew there was no point in stressing himself out, but he sure hoped his mate took everything okay.

Upon reaching Nathan's address, Khan took in the small home with shaker-style siding. There was a small cement front porch where Nathan had hung a large hanging chair. The place had an attached garage that appeared to be an addition because the small second story was on the other side of the house. A dormer faced the opposite direction of the garage and looked into the woods.

As Khan walked up to the house, his attention once again fell on the porch swing. While it wasn't overly large, due to his own small size, he bet they could both fit on it.

If we cuddled.

Giving himself a mental smack upside the head, Khan reminded himself that he should not be thinking that way. He was there to tell his mate that he couldn't claim him right away. Khan actually wondered if Nathan would even be willing to bottom for him. His mate seemed pretty dominant, after all.

Maybe this whole claiming and bonding stress is a moot point, anyway.

"Are you going to ring the bell?" Yuma asked gently. "Or knock?"

The penguin shifter was shorter and smaller than Khan's own five-foot-ten, but Khan definitely envied the other shifter's obvious confidence.

"Or would you like one of us to do it?" Yuma offered, touching his elbow.

Man up, Khan.

"No," Khan responded, perhaps a little sharply. "I'll do it."

Yuma didn't appear offended as he just smiled and nodded.

Focusing on the doorbell button, Khan lifted his hand. He saw it tremble, so he clenched a fist, stuck out his pointer finger, and stabbed the button. His finger instantly hurt a little, telling him he'd jammed it way too hard. Khan heard the chime echo through the house, and he felt grateful he hadn't accidentally broken the button.

That would have been embarrassing.

They waited for a good moment without hearing anything. There was absolutely no sound of movement inside.

Glancing behind him, Khan asked, "Should I, uh, should I hit it again?"

"Absolutely," Yuma responded with an encouraging grin.

"Then we could try knocking," Ryan offered from where he leaned against his motorcycle.

Khan nodded and rang the bell again, pushing it a little more gently that time. Again, he received no response. Blowing out a frustrated breath, Khan made a fist and knocked.

When Khan still didn't receive a response, he turned back to Sam and spread his arms. "Um, now what?"

Hunter stood with his arm slung over Yuma's shoulders and asked, "And today is his day off, right?"

Sam nodded. "Yes. That's what Sheriff Anthony said."

With a hum, Ryan straightened and began jogging around the side of the garage. He came back a minute later. With a shake of his head, Ryan told them, "Bad news. His pick-up isn't in the garage." The enhanced human crossed his arms and squinted at the sky. "Any ideas as to where he may have gone?"

"Eh, this early?" Hunter rested his free hand on his hip. "After working several days, most people would spend the morning cleaning, then the afternoon running errands." He shrugged. "At least, that's how I used to do it."

"When he left, he said he was going to find answers on how to clear out the hunters," Sam stated slowly, squinting at the ground as if searching his memory. The move made the scar on his left cheek pull oddly, accentuating the old mark. "Could he have gone to visit Anthony and he not tell us?"

"Has anyone talked to Anthony since last night?" Ryan asked.

Sam pulled out his phone and dialed the sheriff's number.

"Hey, Sam," Sheriff Anthony greeted. With his shifter hearing, Khan easily heard him, especially as Sam had put the man on speaker. "How's it going? Is Nathan taking everything okay?"

"Last night, Nathan seemed to take things pretty well," Sam told the sheriff. "He even seemed open to a relationship with Khan, but we've run into a snag."

"A snag?" Anthony's sigh came through the line loudly. "Isn't there always. Let me guess. Some sort of miscommunication between Nathan and Khan?"

Sam glanced toward Khan, his expression uneasy. "Uh, something like that. He wouldn't happen to be with you, would he?"

Snorting, Anthony quipped, "Uh, if Nathan was with me, I wouldn't have asked how things went last night. I would have already known."

Lifting his attention to the heavens with a pained look on his face, Sam muttered, "Right, right. Sorry." He licked his full lips before admitting, "We're at Nathan's house, but he's not here. Think we should wander around town looking for him running errands or something?"

From that comment, Khan guessed Sam was grasping at straws.

"Why don't you tell me what the misunderstanding was first?" Anthony asked slowly. "I mean, if he's trying to get relationship advice, he does have a sister an hour away. Depending on how late it was, he may have gone to her."

"A sister?" Khan squeaked. "He can't tell his sister anything."

Sam lifted his hand to stall anymore of Khan's worried ramblings. "He talked about getting information on how to deal with the hunters in the area." Eyeing Khan, Sam continued, "Khan freaked out a little about them and ran off last night, so he may be of the mind that to help Khan settle, he needs to deal with them."

That wasn't the first time Khan had heard those words, but they still caused him to break out in a cold sweat. He didn't want his mate anywhere near those types of murdering bastards.

"Well, if he wanted information on possible hunters, he wouldn't have come to me," Anthony admitted. "All my information is second-hand. I get it from Declan."

Sam frowned. "But you have it, right?"

"Aaaand after realizing why I sent him out there, Nathan may have been a little annoyed with me," Anthony admitted. "Try the alpha. Maybe he's seen him."

Even though Khan was sure Sam knew that Anthony couldn't see it, he still nodded. "Thanks, Anthony," he muttered before disconnecting the line. After inhaling deeply, Sam dialed another number.

After a couple of rings, a deep, lilting voice answered, "Good morning, Beta Sam. I think I know why ye're calling."

While Sam arched a brow, he kept his voice respectful and even. "I hope so, Alpha." He again pinned his attention on Khan. "We're looking for Deputy Nathan Kaldwell. He's not at home."

"Khan's mate. Aye." Declan sounded amused. "He's sleepin' on my office sofa right now."

"Why?" Khan burst out before he could control himself.

"Who's that?" Declan asked cooly.

"I'm sorry, Alpha Declan," Sam quickly stated, obviously attempting to soothe things over. "That's Khan. We're at Nathan's empty house, and he's naturally worried about his mate." Sam clicked the phone off speaker and started walking toward his motorcycle as he brought the phone to his ear. "Is Nathan okay?"

While Khan desperately wanted to know the status of his mate, he realized that Sam taking the phone off speaker meant he wanted privacy. He resisted the urge to follow and bowed his head. A tremble worked through him as his wolf howled softly in the back of his mind, wanting information on their mate.

His wolf was not on board with Khan's decision.

Feeling a slender arm wrap around his waist, Khan blinked twice, refocusing his vision. He met Yuma's gaze, and the other man gave him a smile and a squeeze. Then Yuma began guiding him toward the motorcycles.

Khan realized that everyone had already mounted up, and he wondered how long he'd been zoned out on Nathan's porch.

Without a word, Sam handed Khan his helmet and waited for him to get situated. He wondered at the big shifter's relaxed expression. Khan didn't know how the man could be so confident while heading to the house of another alpha.

Weren't there protocols for that?

Khan couldn't imagine the beta of his old pack heading over to another alpha's house without the pack alpha with him, no matter the situation.

It just wasn't done.

Twisting his fingers together uneasily, Khan watched the trees whirl by once more. He didn't really see them, though. Instead, Khan let his imagination play out all sorts of reasons why Alpha Declan had kept Nathan over at his house the prior night.

Please, don't let him have been hurt by the alpha or something.

Feeling a hand on his nape, Khan looked up to see Sam giving him half his attention. "I can scent your panic and fear, Khan," the big beta rumbled. He had to let go of him to shift gears, then immediately returned his hand to the back of Khan's neck and massaged gently. "Try to relax, little wolf. Declan said that your mate is fine. He was just tired."

Following Sam's urging, Khan nodded and began to do just that. He took long, slow, deep breaths. The feel of the wind on his face, coupled with Sam's occasional squeezes to his neck, helped, too.

Khan was beginning to feel calm again when Sam released him to turn into a driveway. Seeing a large lodge-style home come into view, he tried to disguise his gasp. The place was gorgeous, with stone halfway up the first-story wall, followed by wood paneling the rest of the way. There was a large stone porch with several rockers out front.

Then Khan found his gaze riveted to the old pick-up parked off to the side that he'd seen at their place the prior evening.

My mate is here.

With his wolf's increasing excitement building in his mind, Khan hoped he would be able to stick to his guns. He had to do everything possible to keep his mate away from hunters. They were vicious, and no one ever knew exactly what lengths they would go to to get what they wanted — namely, shifter pelts.

When Sam stopped, Khan quickly shucked his helmet and climbed from the sidecar. He followed the beta up the walk, nerves firing through him at the prospect of facing an alpha wolf. Khan fought against his desire to strip, shift, and run away.

I can do this. For my mate, I can do this.

Then the door began to open just as they reached it, and he spotted the huge African American standing there waiting.

I can't do this.

With a squeak, Khan slipped off his jacket as he stumbled backward a step. He grabbed the hem of his shirt, but before he could whip it over his head, strong arms wrapped around his torso. For an instant, Khan wriggled in their grip, trying to break free.

Then his holder's scent hit his senses.

Nathan.

Oh, so good.

Khan inhaled deeply of Nathan's masculine aroma — so rich and sensual, like a fresh autumn breeze mixed with male musk. Turning his head, he buried his face against Nathan's shirt-clad chest and took another deep breath. A shudder worked through him as he began to relax, and Khan was finally able to make out what Nathan was saying.

"Relax, Khan," Nathan crooned into his ear. "Take a deep breath. That's the way." His mate nuzzled his temple, holding him tight to his chest. "You're okay. You're safe here. No one will ever hurt you, baby. I won't let them." Khan felt Nathan buss a kiss to his temple before whispering, "It's gonna be you and me against the world, baby. You and me forever."

Even knowing what Nathan was asking for — to bond — to twine their life threads — Khan knew he couldn't deny his mate. His mate was asking to be together, and he couldn't say no. Nathan was his mate.

For better or worse, I have to do this.

I have to make my mate happy.

Nothing else matters.

CHAPTER NINE

Nathan had been drinking a morning cup of coffee when he heard the motorcycles pulling up to the house. Seeing Declan rise from the table and head toward the front door, he'd been tempted to join him. Considering this wasn't his house, even though he knew Khan was with the arriving group, Nathan had stayed put.

Then Nathan thought about his skittish little wolf, how he reacted to confrontation, and how intimidating Declan could be.

Setting down his coffee, Nathan rose. He peered toward the front, hesitating.

"Is everything okay?" Lark asked, a mixture of curiosity and concern in his voice. "Need some milk, sugar, or cream for your coffee?"

"Uh, no," Nathan replied with a shake of his head. "I, uh, I think I'm gonna slip around the side."

Nathan ignored Lark's confused look in favor of hurrying out the back door. Rushing around the side of the house, he arrived just in time to see Khan peer up at Declan as he stepped onto the porch. Just as Nathan had worried, Khan appeared to visibly shake with fear before he took a step back and shucked his jacket.

Sprinting forward, Nathan wrapped his arms around Khan before he managed to strip his shirt. He clutched him close and murmured soothing words to the slender male. Recalling how both Kontra and Declan had stressed scents to Nathan, he tucked his mate's nose against his throat.

At first, Nathan worried that the shudder that went through Khan meant he was too late, and his mate was shifting. Then he felt the pretty man sag against him. The wolf shifter snuffled at his throat, taking one deep breath after another.

Nathan held on tight and waited, continuing to murmur soothing words and promises while holding him close around the waist and rubbing his other hand over his back. Over the back of Khan's head, he saw Sam and Declan murmuring together. The other men stood at the base of the deck's steps, watching quietly.

When Khan finally stilled in Nathan's arms, he peered down at him. The shifter rested his forehead against Nathan's shoulder. His hands were clutched in Nathan's shirt at his sides.

Taking a chance, Nathan eased a hand up his back and gently cradled Khan's nape. He used the hold to urge the other man's chin up. Finally, those pretty gray eyes Nathan enjoyed so much met his gaze.

"Hey, baby," Nathan murmured, offering Khan what he hoped was a reassuring smile. "You okay now? You know you're safe here, right?" When Khan just continued to stare at him, Nathan reiterated, "No one here will hurt you. I won't let them. That includes Alpha Declan."

"Y-You c-can't promise that," Khan whispered, his voice cracking a bit. "H-He's the alpha."

Of course, having known Declan in passing for several years—even if he hadn't known the man was the alpha wolf shifter—Nathan felt confident in his assessment.

"Of course I can," Nathan countered, lowering his head a little while continuing to hold Khan's gaze. "Declan's a fair man. Known him for years. Good to work with." With a low chuckle, Nathan added, "Sure, he doesn't suffer fools, but what self-respecting leader would?"

"Wh-What if I-I'm not strong enough?" Khan asked, nibbling his bottom lip.

The move drew Nathan's attention to the plump flesh, making it difficult for him to concentrate on Khan's words.

"Strong enough for what, baby?" Nathan didn't get it.

Khan's brows furrowed as if he didn't understand the question. "A strong enough wolf?" After another shudder passed through him, he admitted, "I'm really not a strong wolf. It's easier to run and hide."

"There's nothing wrong with running and hiding from someone stronger than ye are," Declan cut in softly, having moved close enough to listen in on the conversation. His small smile appeared encouraging. "Fighting a losing battle is only done for two reasons, little one."

"Why?" Khan's voice came out more a squeak.

Declan answered in a low, soothing voice. "One, it's a last resort. Ye have no other option. It's either fight or die." His eyes narrowed, and his tone lowered. "And in that case, ye fight dirty. Pull out every trick ye got to give yerself a chance to get away."

Khan pushed harder into Nathan's hold, and Nathan didn't think the man even realized he was doing it.

"So, fight dirty so I can run away again?" Khan sounded confused as hell, but Declan nodded once in confirmation. "Then what's the other reason."

Declan chuckled. "Because ye're stalling, waiting for help. Waiting for stronger wolves to come save ye."

"No one would ever come help in my old pack," Khan declared, practically breaking Nathan's heart upon hearing the words. "It was every wolf for himself so the alpha would praise you on your strength."

A frown flickered over Declan's countenance for just an instant—there and gone so fast Nathan might have imagined it. Then Declan sported that same small smile again. "Then it's a good thing ye're not part of that pack anymore," he stated with a shrug. He glanced toward Sam, who was standing a step off to the side. "Our packs don't work that way. Here, the pack is family. There are plenty of strong wolves and other shifters who are happy to come to you and yer mate's aid, should ye ever need it." Then Declan held out his hand. "Welcome to me territory, Khan. Ye're welcome here for however long ye like."

"I am?" For a second, Khan stared at Declan's hand as if it were a snake preparing to bite him. Then the look cleared, and he shifted in Nathan's hold just enough so he could reach out and take it. As they shook, Khan whispered, "Why?"

Declan scoffed, releasing Khan's hand. "Because yer mate is here." He waved, indicating Nathan. "After ye secure yer bond, ye'll have to talk about if ye're going to stay or move on with Kontra's people." With another smile, Declan shoved his hands into his pockets. "If ye decide to stay, we'll talk about pack membership at that time."

Damn. Didn't think about that.

Khan was part of a semi-nomadic biker gang. What if he wanted to stay with the group? Nathan was finally feeling settled and comfortable in his life, and he loved his small town. Could he uproot himself if that was what Khan wanted?

One thing at a time. Get him to accept me. Maybe he'd like to be settled, too.

"Um, o-okay," Khan mumbled.

Declan focused on Nathan and patted him on the shoulder. "Good instincts, you coming out here, Nathan." With a wry smirk, he added, "No wonder ye're a good deputy. Ye'd make a fantastic addition to any pack." Then Declan tried to look innocent as he refocused on Khan, but to Nathan, the expression fell flat. "Speakin' of packs, what one did ye hale from, little one?"

Maybe Khan bought the whole innocent act, or maybe it was because such a strong alpha wolf was asking. Either way,

Khan answered, "The Bay River pack in Illinois. Uh, Alpha Darrik Mortin was in charge when I was, uh, when he s-sold . . . me." He finished the last few words on a whisper.

Nathan wasn't the only one who sucked in a sharp breath.

"He sold ye?" Declan growled. "To who?"

Khan pressed closer into Nathan's hold even as he whispered, "The witches . . . for protection against hunters."

"Oh, for the love of—" Declan began before ending with a few colorful expletives. The alpha wolf must have noticed the trembles that once more began in Khan's body, for he rested his hand on Khan's nape and declared, "Khan, no one here is going to sell ye. Not to anyone. Just like yer mate said, ye're safe here."

Nathan noticed the way Declan massaged Khan's neck, and he continued to hold the fearful man. Slowly, the trembles ebbed. Khan sighed, the warm breath fanning against Nathan's neck, causing the hairs to stand on end.

Despite the tense situation, that wasn't the only thing that was beginning to stand up on Nathan. He couldn't seem to help it. The feel of holding the man in his arms was just too wonderful. Khan's lean, five-foot-ten frame fit absolutely perfectly along Nathan's taller, broader body.

"Thank you, Alpha," Khan whispered.

Declan dipped his chin in a curt nod. "Ye're welcome, little one," he stated as he removed his hand. Then he cast a knowing smile in Nathan's direction and said, "I suppose ye'll be heading out then. You and Khan have things to discuss."

Nathan appreciated the man's words, even if they were a dismissal. "Yes, sir. Thanks again for the chat last night."

"Ye're welcome, Nathan," Declan replied, taking a step backward. He started to turn toward Sam. "Don't be a stranger now." Without another word to them, Declan began striding toward the house with Sam and Ryan joining them.

Yuma hung back long enough to confirm that Khan was

okay. Then he and Hunter followed into the house, too.

Alone with Khan for the first time, Nathan suddenly felt a mixture of nerves and arousal. "Can I, uh—" He paused and cleared his throat. "Can I take you to my house?" Nathan watched as Khan tipped his head up, noticing how his lower lip was caught between his teeth. With his focus riveted on the arresting sight, Nathan couldn't help the huskiness of his voice when he murmured, "I'd like the chance to get to know you better."

While Nathan meant talking, sort of, he didn't miss that there was a bit of innuendo in there, either.

Considering the way Khan dipped his head and peered at him through his lashes, Nathan knew the other man had caught it, too.

"O-Okay," Khan agreed.

Nathan wasn't going to ask for confirmation. He didn't want to give Khan a chance to change his mind or succumb to some other fear. With the desire to get Khan in his home surging through him, Nathan turned their hold and began walking toward his truck.

Nathan had never been happier to have remembered to shove his keys, wallet, and phone into his pockets before leaving Declan's study that morning. He pulled his keys out and opened the passenger side door. After helping Khan onto the bench seat, Nathan carefully shut the door and hurried to the other side.

After inserting the keys into the ignition, Nathan turned to face Khan. "There's just one thing I want before we go."

"What?" Khan twisted his hands in his lap, betraying his nerves.

Nathan reached out and rested his left hand on Khan's, stopping his movements. Cradling the other man's jaw with his right, he focused on Khan's swollen bottom lip. He wanted a taste of that so damn badly.

"Can I kiss you?" Nathan asked huskily, his need and de-sire bleeding through his tone.

Khan's breath seemed to catch in his chest. His eyes wid-ened as the gray darkened a little, betraying that he felt the same burning need. His next words shocked Nathan.

"I-I've never been kissed before."

Letting out a soft groan, Nathan asked, "Never?" When Khan shook his head, Nathan asked for clarification. "No man? Or woman either?"

"No one." Khan's face flushed, and he tried to duck his head, but Nathan's hold wouldn't let him. "Wh-What if I'm no good?"

"Oh, baby." Nathan hated how Khan's first instinct was to be afraid of something. "Not possible." He vowed to help the sweet little man change that. "Let me show you how good it will be."

Khan met Nathan's gaze again, his attention roving over his face to finally settle on his lips. "Okay."

That one softly whispered word sent a wealth of desire and need flooding Nathan's body. The trust Khan was giving him, to take a leap of faith that Nathan would make it good, was such a rush. Nathan would do everything in his power to ful-fill that promise.

As Nathan closed the distance between their mouths, an-other thought hit him, causing his cock to throb in his jeans.

If Khan's never been kissed, does that mean he's just as innocent in every area of intimacy?

Chapter Ten

A s Nathan's face drew closer to his own, Khan's heart rate
spiked, anticipation thrumming through him. He'd
never had a chance to get close to anyone. Everything about
his old pack was all about posturing and power, and it'd been
so much easier to run rather than look for a connection of any
kind.

Even sex between couples had been about power and ma-
nipulation. He'd seen other shifters go at it, then use the
knowledge to gain rank or to blackmail, and he'd wanted
nothing to do with any of it.

With Nathan, however, his handsome mate, Khan wanted
to try . . . so very badly.

To Khan's surprise, Nathan turned his head at the last second and nuzzled his cheek against Khan's own. The light
scratch of his morning fuzz sent tingles down his neck, and
he gasped as the hairs on his arms stood on end. The move
was such a shifter thing that his wolf rumbled happily in his
mind, taking that as his mate marking him.

"Oh, baby," Nathan rumbled softly, the warmth of his
breath teasing at Khan's ear. "I'll kiss every inch of your body
at some point, beautiful," his mate whispered huskily. "And
I'm honored to give you your first kiss."

Then Nathan turned his head and pressed his lips lightly
against the corner of Khan's mouth in the gentlest of caresses.
He lifted, then moved to the other corner of his mouth. Nathan licked along Khan's lower lip before suckling lightly at
the flesh.

Khan gasped at the stimulus, the play sending zings down his chest, and his nipples beaded, tingling pleasantly.

"Oh, yessss," Nathan hissed quietly before finally sealing his mouth over Khan's fully. Nathan dipped his tongue between his lips, teasing at Khan's own. Pulling away, Nathan stared deep into Khan's eyes as he urged, "Just follow my lead and enjoy, baby."

Nathan slid his fingers up his neck and threaded them into Khan's hair. Using the hold, he tugged the strands lightly, positioning Khan's head a little to the side. Nathan dipped his head and sealed his mouth over Khan's once more. Then he pushed inside Khan, using his lips and tongue to massage and manipulate Khan's own.

Moaning softly at the exquisite sensations cascading through his body, Khan was only so happy to go along. He lifted his hands and gripped Nathan's shirt. Twisting his fingers in the fabric, he clung to the other man, losing himself in the sensation of Nathan's lips and tongue.

Khan felt his brain shutting down, and his body felt as if it went up in flames. His dick ached within the confines of his jeans, seeming to pulse and twitch in time with Nathan's laps against his tongue. Fiery tendrils coursed through his veins, and he couldn't stop from shifting his hips restlessly as he searched for . . . something.

Suddenly, Nathan tore his lips away from Khan's, letting out a harsh groan.

Khan mewled, worried that he'd done something wrong until Nathan muttered, "God, Khan." He stared down at him with brown eyes that had turned nearly black with his desire. "You're so responsive. I want to suck you off so badly."

Gasping, Khan stared at Nathan in shock. "Y-You do?"

Nathan's nostrils flared as he swept his gaze over Khan's frame. "Oh, yes," he rumbled, his smile turning feral, telling Khan he must have liked what he saw. Then Nathan sobered.

"But we're sitting in front of Alpha Declan's house." His mate grimaced. "I didn't mean for things to get so out of control or to seem like a cock-tease. You just respond so beautifully."

While Khan hated that Nathan had to be the voice of reason, he understood. Even though his dick was hating the pause, he whispered, "I understand." Untangling one hand from Nathan's shirt, Khan smiled up at him as he reached out and traced his fingertips along his human's jaw. "Thank you for my first kiss. It was amazing."

Letting out another groan, Nathan turned his head and nipped at Khan's fingertips. "You're welcome, baby." Then he pulled away and straightened in his seat. As Nathan fired up his truck and started them on their way, he vowed, "And you can be sure we'll be doing plenty more when we reach my house."

Khan nodded, looking forward to that.

As Nathan drove, he stated offhand, as if he were discussing the weather, "By the way, when we get to my place, I expect you to claim me."

"Wh-What?" Khan squeaked. Even as his cock throbbed and his wolf howled in his mind at the idea of claiming Nathan, he sputtered, "B-But, the hunters could target you. Could hurt you if you're connected with a shifter." Then, needing his mate to understand, Khan admitted his greatest fear. "And I don't think I could protect you."

Nathan smiled at him.

Smiled!

"Khan, baby." Nathan continued to smile as he refocused on the road. "I don't know how to say this other than to just be blunt." With a shrug, Nathan claimed, "I don't need you to protect me, nor do I want you to." Before Khan could counter, Nathan reached over and took his hand again, giving it a squeeze. "I know that it's your shifter instincts telling you to keep me safe, and I'm flattered, but I'm a sheriff's deputy. I fight crime and work to keep the peace for a living. I'm very well trained to take care of myself and keep myself safe."

As that information worked its way through Khan's brain, he felt his wolf whine in his mind. Worry flooded him, easing the strain of his boner. He frowned as he opened his mouth, then closed it again, uncertain how to respond. It wasn't as if he would ever dare to ask his mate to quit his work.

Before Khan could hope to come up with something, Nathan continued, "Besides, I intend to help track down these hunters and clear them from the area." He squeezed Khan's hand again. "I want you safe, after all. Now then, would you like me to do that with the benefits of our bonding gifts, increased strength, speed, stamina, and tougher bones? Or should I just do it as a regular ol' human?"

Khan snapped his attention to Nathan's face, taking in the smile there and the twinkle in his human's eyes. It hit him hard and fast. "You're manipulating me, aren't you?"

Nathan stopped his truck at a stop sign and turned to face him. "Perhaps it seems that way, but I don't mean it like that." Squeezing Khan's fingers, he pulled them to his mouth and gave his knuckles a kiss. "What I'm doing is being truthful with my mate. I want you safe in a place where you don't have to be afraid. So I'm going to do my damnedest make that happen." Nathan's deep brown-eyed gaze bored into Khan's. "Will you help me by bonding with me? By moving into my home and staying by my side?" As Khan gaped at him, Nathan smiled. "After all, how can mates keep each other safe, happy, and well-satisfied if they're not together?"

With his heart racing in his chest, Khan took in Nathan's warm yet serious expression. In the face of that logic, he knew his mate was right. The best way for Khan to keep Nathan safe was to be by his side, a bonded couple.

"Okay," Khan finally responded softly. "I-I'd like that."

"Me, too," Nathan replied. After another kiss to Khan's knuckles, he started the truck moving again.

The ride was only another few minutes, and Khan felt his excitement and anticipation ramping up with every second. The cab was quiet except for the sound of the truck's engine and the rumble of tires on asphalt. It wasn't uncomfortable, however. After all, they'd said everything that was important.

We're going to build a life together.

Khan practically vibrated in his seat with the surge of arousal he felt. Except, when they pulled up to the house, a fresh wave of nerves hit as he realized something. He'd never done anything before.

What if I can't please my mate?

"I hear you thinking over there, Khan," Nathan commented as he parked his truck in the garage. After removing the keys from the ignition, he turned to face him. "What's wrong?"

"I've never done anything with anyone before," Khan blurted out.

Nathan nodded once. "You mentioned that about kissing." His expression turned hungry as he narrowed his eyes. "Does that include *everything*?"

Nibbling his bottom lip, Khan nodded.

"I'll show you everything you need to do, baby," Nathan assured, pushing his door open and sliding from the truck. "Come with me, and we'll explore everything together."

Khan sat there a few seconds longer before realizing he needed to trust Nathan.

My mate won't steer me wrong.

Girding up his courage, Khan slid from the pick-up. He closed the door and joined Nathan at the hood. After sliding his hand back into Nathan's, Khan allowed his soon-to-be lover to lead him into the house.

Nathan moved through the house with steady strides, and Khan found his self-confidence an aphrodisiac all on its own. As they passed through the kitchen, Nathan paused to grab a couple of bottles of water from the fridge. With a wink, he told him, "For afterward."

Khan nodded absently.

After. After we have sex. After I've claimed my mate. After we've bonded.

Those thoughts spiraled through his head, making his arousal soar. His dick grew harder with every step, his anticipation growing. Khan realized he'd zoned out when they stopped walking.

"You okay, Khan?" Nathan asked. He'd turned to face him and was resting his hands on his shoulders. His thumbs lightly traced up and down the sides of his neck. "Am I pushing you?"

"A little bit," Khan answered honestly. Seeing Nathan wince, his expression turning crestfallen, he quickly amended, "I do want this. I really do." Placing his hands on Nathan's t-shirt-covered pectorals, Khan quickly added, "I just have no idea what I'm doing."

"Okay." Nathan smiled. "Well, we start by getting naked." Reaching for the hem of his shirt, his mate asked, "Is that okay?"

Khan sucked in a sharp breath as he swept his gaze over the bigger, broader male. "Oh, yes." He wanted to see his mate naked so very badly. "Want to see you."

Nathan grinned. Then he wasted no time in doing exactly as he'd offered. He tugged his shirt over his head, revealing broad shoulders, clearly defined pecs, and beautiful washboard abdominals. Beneath Nathan's belly button was a slender treasure trail that disappeared into his jeans . . . except, not for long. Nathan popped the button, then undid the zipper. He pushed not only his jeans but his underwear, too, down his legs. With a chuckle, he sat on the bed and bent over to remove his boots and socks before kicking off the rest.

Resting on the comforter with his legs slightly splayed, relaxing back on his elbows, Nathan stared up at him. He grinned hotly as he eyed Khan. His beautiful tanned body was on clear display, and Khan couldn't tear his gaze away from the thick cock jutting from Nathan's groin. The way it already leaked a bead of pre-cum caused his mouth to water, and he licked his lips with anticipation.

"Oh, baby. Love the way you're looking at me," Nathan rumbled on a groan. "But you're a little overdressed, Khan."

Khan yanked his attention away from the miles of skin he wanted to touch—to trace his fingers all over. His heart felt as if it would beat right out of his chest. His cock felt so engorged by the arresting view before him, he feared he would come without a touch.

Jerking his clothes from his body, Khan heard a few stitches tearing, but he couldn't bring himself to care. With his wolf driving him—screaming at him to *take, take, take*—he got naked as swiftly as possible. Except, once he stood nude before his human, Khan didn't know what to do, and he paused uncertainly.

"Relax, Khan," Nathan encouraged, realizing his predicament. "I saw you eyeing my cock." He winked as he asked, "Would you like to suck me while I prepare myself for your dick?"

Khan snapped his gaze back to Nathan's erection, and his mouth watered once more. "Yes, please." He really, *really* wanted to taste his mate's pre-cum. Then Khan registered what Nathan had said. "Get yourself ready?"

Nathan nodded. "You have a pretty impressive prick there, Khan." He pointed toward Khan's groin. "I hope to get to suck it soon, but I know to bond, you have to top me, and I'm gonna need to prepare my hole with plenty of lube for you to slide into me safely."

Nodding slowly, Khan figured that made sense. He recalled the guys with Kontra's group talking about lube and prep. Khan felt his cheeks heat as he finally put two and two together and realized they'd been talking about sex.

Gods, I'm such a virgin.

Not for long, though.

"Okay," Khan whispered.

"Don't worry," Nathan vowed as he rolled to his side and opened the nightstand drawer. "I know this seems sort of clinical, but we'll get to the slow explorations after we bond." As Nathan slid up onto the bed on his back, rolling a little on his side as he popped the cap on the lube, he winked at Khan. "It'll take the edge off, then we can get to figuring out all the other things we'll enjoy together."

Khan nodded, deciding to follow Nathan's lead. "Okay," he said again, for want of anything else.

"Okay." Nathan beckoned with his fingers, as if the way he stared at Khan with such lust and need wasn't an invitation in and of itself. "Come on up here, Khan."

Only too happy to comply, Khan climbed onto the bed. With his gaze snagged completely by Nathan's beautiful engorged organ, he settled next to his mate's thigh. Lifting a hand, Khan gently traced the pulsing vein running the length.

"I've never done this before," Khan whispered, glancing up at Nathan's face. "What if I do it wrong?"

Nathan shivered, his nostrils flaring. "Just do what comes natural, Khan." Then he waggled his brows, offering a bit of levity. "Just watch your teeth."

"The only place I'll put my teeth is in your neck."

"Oh, fuck, yeah," Nathan responded with a groan as he reached one hand behind himself. "Can't wait."

Surprised to hear how out of breath Nathan sounded, Khan peered up to find his mate's face and chest flushed. He clearly saw the desire and lust etched on his features. Something settled inside Khan, and he returned his attention to Nathan's cock.

Khan gripped the base and tipped it toward his mouth. Parting his lips, he wrapped them around the head and sucked strongly. His mate's deep masculine flavor burst across his taste buds as he swiped his tongue over the crown, scooping up the bead of pre-cum he'd spotted. Khan hummed appreciatively, relishing the sweet musky flavor, and sucked strongly, hoping for more. Khan sank deep before drawing partway off again. He massaged the man's vein, trying to give as much stimulation as possible as he did it all again.

"Ah, yeah, Khan," Nathan whispered on a groan. "So good. Feels so good." Grunting, he threaded his fingers through Khan's hair, cupping his head and holding him lightly. Nathan began to thrust shallowly. "That's the way, baby. You're a fucking natural."

Peering up at Nathan through his lashes, Khan took in Nathan's expression of feral delight as he watched him take his cock. Seeing his mate's pleasure ramped up Khan's own, and he sucked harder on Nathan's delicious length, being careful to keep his teeth covered.

"Shit," Nathan hissed. He tightened his grip on Khan's hair and used the hold to pull him away. "Fuck me now, Khan," he demanded. "Need you now."

Khan's erection, which he'd been doing his best to ignore, twitched as he heard the need in Nathan's voice. As soon as Khan pulled off his mate's prick, Nathan stretched out the leg he'd had cocked up and spread his thighs. Khan quickly got into position, his wolf urging him onward.

Once Khan was between Nathan's thighs, his mate reached up and gripped his dick. Khan moaned, his eyelids sliding shut as blissful tingles danced up his spine. Feeling the lube being slathered on him, Khan sucked in a sharp breath, barely hanging on.

When Nathan pulled his hand away, Khan didn't know if he wanted to moan from relief or frustration.

"Come on, baby," Nathan urged roughly. "Sink that beautiful dick of yours in me. Come claim your mate."

Khan needed no further urging. Gripping the base of his cock, he guided his head to Nathan's prepared hole. He felt the softened muscle pushing against his crown . . . and thrust.

Sinking into the hot vice of Nathan's body, Khan gasped in shock. The sensations bombarding his system made his head swim. As Khan pushed in and in and in, his breathing became ragged. Staring down where his shaft speared his mate, seeing them connected so intimately, Khan finally understood the bliss of sharing with the other half of his soul. He felt his balls roll, and he whined as he tried to hold off his orgasm just from the initial push in.

"It's okay, Khan," Nathan crooned into his ear, wrapping his arms around him and pulling him flush to his chest. After nipping at his chin, he encouraged, "Just let go, my shifter. Stop thinking. Just let your instincts go."

That encouragement was all it took.

Khan groaned, giving in. He pulled his hips back once, twice, then slammed into Nathan's gripping heat. His orgasm surged through him as hot blissful fire coursed through his veins. Groaning Nathan's name, Khan coated Nathan's innards, marking him in a deep primitive way.

Even as Khan floated on the heady bliss of endorphins, his wolf howled in the back of his mind. With a moan, he let the beast take over. His canines lengthened, he leaned forward, and he sank them deep into the flesh of Nathan's shoulder.

"Khan!"

Hearing Nathan's shout, Khan feared he'd hurt his mate. As his mate's life-blood flowed across his tongue and he suckled over the wound, he nearly pulled free. Then Khan heard Nathan's groan, the sound one of pleasure and satisfaction. The heat of Nathan's release, warming the space between them, reassured him further.

I pleased my mate. Claimed him. Mine forever.

With that knowledge, Khan eased his teeth free, licked the would clean, and relaxed across his lover's torso.

Nathan chuckled huskily beneath him as he skimmed his palms over Khan's backside. "Damn, baby," he mumbled, his words slightly slurred. "That claiming bite is fuckin' awesome." Nathan pecked a kiss to his temple before mumbling sleepily, "You can do that to me anytime."

Khan smiled as he whispered, "Okay."

CHAPTER ELEVEN

Nathan whistled as he pulled open the front door to the sheriff's department. Spotting Markus at the front desk, he cut off the sound and narrowed his eyes. Unable to help himself, Nathan crossed his arms over his chest and paused beside him.

Markus's dark eyes widened a little as he sniffed none-too-discreetly. "Uh, hey, Nathan," he greeted. While a smile toyed around his lips, there was also a hint of uncertainty in his eyes. "How are ya, man?"

"Good, no thanks to you," Nathan replied gruffly. "Thanks for hangin' me out to dry a couple nights ago."

It was Markus's turn to scowl. "What are you talking about?"

"The wellness check that you didn't back me up on, Markus," Nathan stated pointedly. "Remember?" He lifted his phone from the holder at his belt and wiggled it. "I never contacted you about the outcome, and you never followed up. Hung. Me. Out . . . to dry." With a curl of his lip, Nathan declared, "I outta report you for that."

"Oh, come on, Nathan." Markus rolled his eyes, even as a flush worked up his cheeks. His voice even took on a hint of a whine. "You weren't in any danger."

Unable to hold onto his ire, Nathan grinned broadly as he barked a laugh. "Just givin' ya shit, man." He rounded the desk and punched him on the upper arm. "Couldn't resist."

"Asshole," Markus growled softly, but there wasn't any heat in it. Instead, he rose to his feet and gave Nathan a quick bro-hug. "Welcome to our world."

"Thanks, buddy," Nathan responded, slapping him on the back. "It's been an interesting couple of days off, that's for sure."

Markus snickered. "Guess I'll still be seein' ya after I *retire*." He lifted his hands, making air quotes.

"Why are you saying retire like that?" Nathan asked curiously, stepping away from the other deputy. Then he widened his eyes as it clicked. "Oh." Lowering his voice, Nathan guessed, "You're gonna have to go on that mandatory hiding out period, aren't you?"

Nodding, Markus kept his voice just as low even though they were the only two people in the room. "Yup. It's my time."

"You'll be missed around here," Nathan told him honestly.

"Thanks."

Nathan offered a wave as he headed toward the back so he could get his shift started.

Although Nathan had spent three days in bed and around the house with Khan, he realized he already missed the man, and he'd only been on shift for an hour. He'd gotten a call from Sheriff Anthony that first afternoon, giving him time off to properly get to know the wolf shifter. Nathan sure had appreciated that, and they'd spent the time getting comfortable with each other.

Nathan smiled, recalling his phone call with his sister the prior evening. He hadn't wanted her to find out that he was starting a relationship from anyone other than himself. She hadn't batted an eye that it was with a man. Instead, she'd expressed concern that Nathan was moving Khan in so swiftly.

His response had been, "I just know it's right."

After another word of caution, she'd wished him well.

Then she'd asked when Nathan was going to bring Khan around to meet them all.

"Oh, Deputy Nathan!"

Nathan turned upon hearing Maddy call his name. Seeing that he was already in the alley behind the stores, he mentally winced. He'd been making his rounds without paying any attention to what was going on around him.

Can't be doin' that.

After the mental chastisement, Nathan smiled at Maddy. "Good morning, Maddy," he greeted. "How are you this fine morning?"

Maddy laughed, her blue eyes twinkling. "Well, someone is in a good mood today." She gave him a cheeky smile as she asked, "There a reason for that, deputy?"

"As a matter of fact, there is," Nathan replied, unable to contain his happiness. "Remember when we talked about how I'd know when I met the right one last week?"

"Oh, my, yes." Maddie offered him a knowing grin. "I know it wasn't my Cindy, so who's this special someone?"

"His name's Khan, and he's—" Nathan paused and barked a laugh. "Well, I was gonna say perfect, but no one's perfect." Nathan shrugged, smiling as he thought of his lover. "Still, we mesh."

"Mesh?" Maddy teased, waggling her eyebrows teasingly. "Is *that* what young people are calling it these days?"

Nathan chuckled, fighting against the heat threating to creep up his neck. "So." He cleared his throat, trying to switch gears. Recalling that she'd hollered for him, Nathan asked, "Was there something I could help you with today?"

"Oh, yes." Maddy chuckled. "Nearly forgot." Her expression sobered, her lips pursing. "My Cindy is moving here, and she was supposed to look at a house today." Resting her hands on her hips, Maddy frowned. "Her realtor, Witney Risney, called this morning and canceled, saying that the house wasn't ready to be shown inside yet, but she was curious about the place, see?"

Nodding, Nathan wondered where she was going with this.

"So, Cindy went out there and found the place." Maddy's face darkened as she scowled. "That realtor was there with another group."

"Ahh, I'm sorry, Maddy," Nathan stated in commiseration. "Sounds like she undercut your granddaughter with a different buyer."

Maddy shook her head. "No, that's just it. Cindy parked and started walkin' up, wanting to talk to Witney, but then she heard what was bein' said." Unease entered Maddy's expression, and she began twisting her fingers together. "Cindy told me that Whitney told a man she couldn't just take one of her clients' homes off the market without notice. He should have called and given her time to make arrangements." Growing more animated, Maddy continued, "The guy said that, *with what I pay you to look the other way, you can figure out what to tell your client. Just make it happen.*" Maddy's eyes had grown wide, and her cheeks were flushed. "Whitney agreed, but said she would expect a bonus for fixing his screw-up. Well, he called her a, well, a female dog"—Maddie drew close, lowering her voice—"if you know what I mean."

Nathan nodded, not liking what he was hearing at all.

Could a drug or gun runner be setting up a base of operations in Stone Ridge?

Not on my watch.

"Is Cindy okay?" Nathan asked, worry filling him. "Did they see her?"

"Oh, Cindy's fine, don't you worry." Maddy reached over and patted his arm. "After that, she got out of there and came straight here to me." Pointing in the house, Maddy asked, "She's pretty shook up, but when I saw you out here walkin', I wanted to let you know as soon as possible."

"This just happened this morning?"

Maddy nodded. "Mmm-hmm."

"Do you know the address?" Nathan hoped if he hurried out there, he could spot something suspicious.

"Here you go." Maddy held out a slip of paper.

"Thank you, Maddy." Nathan gripped her upper arm in a light grip, expressing his appreciation. "One of us will check it out right away."

Maddy nodded again. "Thank you, deputy."

"Thank you," Nathan countered before turning and starting back the way he'd come. At the same time, Nathan reached up, activated his microphone, and indicated the code for suspicious activity. "Permission to head out there and check it out."

"Granted." Nereo's voice came through the line, telling Nathan that the vampire was on dispatch. "Keep me posted on if you need back-up."

"Will do."

Nathan hurried to a cruiser and climbed inside. After punching in the code to access the vehicle's spare key lock box, he fired up the vehicle. With adrenaline fueling him, Nathan entered the address into the vehicle's GPS and headed that way.

Winding his way deeper and deeper into the mountains, Nathan realized the address was really close to where Kontra and his people were holed up. He eased off on his cruiser's gas pedal as he closed in on his destination. Spotting a dirt road only a quarter of a mile from the address, Nathan pulled into it and parked.

Using the cruiser's microphone, Nathan reported that he'd arrived close to the address and was proceeding on foot. It took a moment for Nereo to finally respond by saying to proceed with caution. Nathan rolled his eyes even as he confirmed.

Exiting his cruiser, Nathan started through the woods toward the nearby house. He crept along, watching for any movement. To his surprise, Nathan spotted a tripwire in a tree.

Yep. Definitely suspicious.

Nathan quickly called it in. Nereo ordered him to back off until back-up arrived. Agreeing, Nathan began easing away from the property.

Before Nathan made it back to the cruiser, he heard movement in the trees to his left. He froze, crouching quickly. Knowing how close he was to Alpha Kontra's people, Nathan wondered for an instant if it was a shifter out running. If so, he could unwittingly blow an operation.

Pulling out his phone, Nathan quickly fired off a text to Sam. *Are any of your people running three miles northwest of your house?* Nathan just hoped Sam was in human form and could respond quickly.

To Nathan's relief, he was.

No. A few guys headed south, but not north. Why?

Nathan didn't mind sharing with the big beta. After all, he needed to warn them away from the area until they figured out what was going on.

Got suspicious activity at an address close to you.

After hitting send, he added the address in question and hit send again. Then he added a warning.

Best stay clear.

For a moment, Nathan thought that would be it. A second later, he received another text.

Need help?

Before Nathan could answer in the negative, movement caught his attention. He barely refrained from hissing when he spotted the blond wolf ease from between two trees. Fortunately, the animal wasn't looking his way.

Acting on instinct, Nathan lifted his phone and snapped a picture. He added it to his text, asking, *Know this wolf?*

Nope. Want me to ask Declan?

Yes, thanks.

After Nathan fired off that message, he returned his focus to the wolf. Except, he didn't see it. Cussing mentally, Nathan searched earnestly for some sign of the wolf.

The growl from his left told Nathan what he wanted to know. Except, it wasn't good news. Turning just his head, Nathan found the wolf standing ten feet away from him. The blond wolf's lips were peeled back from his teeth, his ears were pinned back, and angry-sounding growls issued from his throat.

"Well, fuck." Nathan whispered the words as he searched the wolf's eyes. During his discussions with Kontra and Declan, they'd both confirmed that the only wolves in the area were shifters. They'd also explained how sacred fated mates were to them. Trusting in that, Nathan licked his lips before saying, "I'm a fated mated to a wolf shifter. I'm not a danger to you."

For an instant, the wolf didn't respond.

Nathan began to wonder if he would be able to reach his firearm before the wolf pounced on him.

A second later, the wolf stopped growling. It tipped its head up a bit and sniffed. Then the shifter began to change. The familiar sound of muscles popping, bones cracking, and tendons snapping filled the woods.

Nathan took the opportunity of the shifter being slightly disoriented from changing to unsnap the safety guard on his gun . . . just in case.

A blond man finally began to rise to his feet. There was a smile on his face, and as Nathan had learned, he didn't seem at all worried about his nudity. Resting his hands on his hips, the blond looked him up and down.

"Hey, deputy," the guy greeted. "Sorry to freak you out. I didn't realize one of my packmates had mated recently." Continuing to grin, he asked, "Congrats, man. Who are you with?"

While Nathan wasn't a shifter and couldn't scent truths, there was something in the blond's blue eyes that he just didn't trust. Over the years, he'd learned to trust his deputy instincts. Besides, Nathan would bet his left nut that if a wolf in Declan or Kontra's pack spotted a human they didn't know, they would flee, not approach and confront.

"Khan," Nathan answered, knowing he had to be honest.

"Yeah?" The wolf shifter seemed just a little too interested. "Khan what?"

Digging deep into his bullshit ability, and the adage that you're not lying if you believe what you say, Nathan told him, "No last name, yet. He's new to the area." He pointed at his neck where his mating mark was hiding under his uniform collar. "Hence me being newly mated to him, and you not hearing about it yet. Just a few days new." Nathan offered a wide grin of his own as he added, "Declan's offered to talk to him about membership." Trying to stay loose and relaxed, Nathan asked, "I'm Deputy Nathan Kaldwell. What's your name?"

Just as Nathan had suspected, the blond openly scented him again. "I'm Nick Greely. A tracker for Declan."

Odd. Wouldn't he call him Alpha Declan?

"Good to meet you, Nick," Nathan offered, thinking quickly. "I hear your pack plays poker a lot. I'd love to get in on that." That was true enough. Nathan did like to play a hand of friendly poker. "Maybe I'll see you there."

"Lies." A deep lilted voice that Nathan recognized as Alpha Declan McIntire echoed through the trees, making the blond tense. "So many lies." The dark-skinned alpha appeared between the trees, flanked by Alpha Kontra. "But I will say I'm so happy to see ye, Larson." Declan chuckled coldly. "Never thought ye'd actually be dumb enough to come back here."

Payson walked out of the trees, naked as the day he was

born. Obviously, he'd been doing something in his hyena form. The guy's grin appeared feral as he pinned it on the shifter Declan had called Larson. It was obvious that Payson wasn't impressed with the wolf.

"Guy's setting up a gun runnin' business through here," Payson claimed, sneering at Larson. "Thinks cause you like everythin' quiet, if they stay under the radar, it'll be nice and secure here." Giving the guy a withering look, Payson added, "He's also the one who occasionally let's hunters know you're here. That way, you're kept busy with *them*." The hyena shifter practically spat the words, his anger was so near the surface. "And you'll be too busy to notice him and his stooges."

"Hmmm, good to know," Declan slowly stalked toward Larson. "Ye've caused all kinds of problems, Larson." His smile turned feral. "Or should I say . . . *rogue*."

Larson snarled. "You don't deserve this pack." Before he'd even started speaking, Larson began shifting.

Declan didn't even bother trying to remove the sweat shorts he was wearing. Lunging forward, he changed from man to wolf in midair, his boots falling from his rear paws. A second later, Declan's large chocolate wolf landed on the half-shifted Larson.

Blood sprayed across the trees as Declan ripped out Larson's throat without even a growl of warning.

Declan took a couple of steps backward, his tail sticking out of a shorts leg awkwardly, but he didn't seem to care. After watching the downed shifter for several seconds, he changed back into human form. Once Declan had straightened his shorts on his hips, he accepted the cloth from Kontra and wiped his mouth.

"We owe you our thanks, Nathan," Declan began, his voice a little muffled. Casting a curled-lip sneer at the dead shifter, he shook his head. When Declan returned his focus to Nathan, his expression cleared. "We've been after this rogue for a couple of years now. Yer picture to Sam was invaluable."

Nathan dipped his chin in a nod. "Between the weird activity reported at this address and the fact that I'm sure one of your shifters would have fled, not confronted, I thought there was something fishy about him," he admitted. Rubbing the back of his neck, he frowned. "Glad a rogue's out of commission, as well as him being the guy who's been sharing your location with hunters."

"You have no idea," Declan murmured, letting out a long sigh. Just that fast, there seemed to be a weight off the alpha wolf's shoulder. He smiled at Nathan. "We're in yer debt."

Even as Nathan figured there was a story there, he shook his head. "Nope. No debt," he countered. Lifting his hands in placation when the alpha's black brows shot up, he told him, "Fighting crime is my job, and my pack is now part of my family." Nathan grinned. "We fight for family."

Declan smiled widely. "Family, eh? You and Khan have decided to stay?"

Nathan nodded. "We have."

He and Khan had talked about it the prior night, but they hadn't taken the time to discuss it with either alpha. They'd been too busy taking care of each other's needs.

Kontra grinned and patted Nathan on his back. "We'll miss Khan, but we're happy for you both." Then he winked and added, "When you're ready for a new life identity, look us up. We'll still be around."

Nathan thought of his *Harley Street Glide* in his garage at home and nodded. "Thanks, Alpha Kontra. I bet we'll take you up on that."

"Call for you." Declan handed Nathan his phone.

"Deputy Nathan here."

Sheriff Anthony's voice came over the line. "Heard what happened out there, Nathan. Great instincts."

"Thank you, sheriff."

Damn. News travels fast with shifters.

"You're welcome," Anthony replied. Then, to Nathan's surprise, his boss ordered, "Now go home. You have a mate to soothe."

More than happy to do just that, Nathan agreed. "Thank you, sheriff." Then he remembered the rest of Maddy's report. "Oh, Larson was paying off realtor Whitney Risney in some way. Probably for information on where empty houses in the area were," he guessed. "I don't know if she knows about shifters, but she's dirty."

Anthony growled softly before saying, "Got it. We'll take care of it on this end. Just get back to Khan for now. Your mate will need to see that you're well after hearing about your encounter with a rogue."

"Thanks again, Sheriff," Nathan replied.

After handing Declan his phone, Nathan began jogging through the woods back to his cruiser. Parked next to his cruiser was Sam on his motorcycle. The beta held out a helmet while pointing to the sidecar.

"I'll take you," the beta stated.

Grinning, Nathan tucked the cruiser's key back into the lock box, then joined the beta, happy for the ride.

A few minutes later, what was even better, was Khan standing on his porch, eagerly awaiting his arrival.

Nathan strode up his porch steps and swept Khan into his arms. His shifter jumped, wrapping his arms and legs around his waist. While noticing the sound of a few chuckles, Nathan ignored them.

Instead, Nathan carried Khan into their house. Having every intention of spending the evening expending his excess adrenaline by pounding his shifter into the mattress, he carried his mate into the bedroom. Nathan slowly lowered Khan to the bed, then followed him down.

Kissing Khan, Nathan basked in the knowledge that he and

his wolf were right where they were meant to be.

ABOUT THE AUTHOR

Charlie started writing fantasy when she was eight, and after stumbling onto her first erotic romance at age nineteen, she realized her true calling. She now focuses on writing gay erotic romance, normally of the paranormal variety, with heroes of all kinds. With the help and support of her husband, Charlie finally fulfilled one of her life-long goals . . . move to acreage with her horses. You can often find her curled up with her laptop and a cup of tea or glass of wine, creating her next adventure. Charlie enjoys exploring the mountains of her new Oregon home on horseback, 4-wheeler, or motorcycle.

She can be reached at ch.richards2010@yahoo.com

Or visit her at www.charlie-richards.com.